Amelia Earhart, Serial Killer

Serial Women of History Series

Amanda Byrd

Blacksheep Press, LLC

Contents

About the Author

Amanda Byrd is obsessed with fictional serial killers. From Patrick Bateman to Dr. Hannibal Lecter to Dexter Morgan and every butcher in between, Amanda loves figuring out what drives fiction's deadliest monsters. When she's not busy writing, Amanda can be found reading, playing video games, or watching shows and movies like Mindhunter, Hannibal, and Dexter. She lives in Florida with her bloodthirsty, flesh-eating cat.

Follow Amanda online
www.amandabyrd.net

Sign up for my newsletter and get a free story

Follow Amanda online:
Facebook: Author Amanda Byrd
Instagram: amanda_byrd_author
Goodreads: Amanda Byrd
Bookbub: Amanda Byrd

One

I SHOULDN'T HAVE BEEN there. Atchison was a small town, and it felt as though the whole world knew who I was. As much as she and I didn't get along, she was still my mother. And she deserved the respect. She deserved to hear me say it.

"Amy—mother—you passed thinking I was dead. For that, I apologize. I came back to thank you for bringing me into existence. Goodbye."

I knew I had to keep it short. Sweet, however, was another issue altogether, for there was always the feeling that she resented the adoration I held for my father. And that I was such a daring girl, lady, and woman.

I turned on my heel, pulling the black veil down over my face as I walked away from Amy's grave. There were no tears in my eyes, no sadness in my heart for her no longer being here. There was only anger and frustration.

My father, Edwin, was not buried here with her, as he should have been. His ashes had been buried in Forest Lawn, Glendale, California. Alone, with no family. It was my intention to go there. To tell him my adventures which lead me home. To tell him of the daughter he created, the one hiding for 42 years.

Avoiding my sister, Muriel, would be much easier there. She would die of shock if she found out I was actually alive; that my death had only been declared. I knew better than to travel near Medford, Massachusetts.

George would not know I was still alive, either. California had only been very good to me for flying, not much else. It was simply easier to live there and take off for my flights... the ones that had not been across the Atlantic, anyway. Going back there was never an intention.

I walked back to the boarding house I had rented a room in, and wrote my final letter to my father in my journal while waiting for the sun to set.

At night, I was not the Amelia Earhart the world knew and loved.

I donned my pajamas and wrote my final letter to my father, grateful he had never come to know who his little girl truly was. Amy and Muriel never suspected anything either. The darkness I'd come to know was a comfort—a friend. I'd learned to embrace it as a young child. To depend on it in my darkest times.

When I was plane-wrecked and lost on that island, that darkness had saved me. Not that I was "lost." I'd staged it all in favor of my dark friend. I'd grown weary of the crowds that gathered around me everywhere I went. Of the lies from George. Of living in "a man's world" and being judged for not

being "ladylike." Hell, George only married me to look better in the eyes of the
public and for the sponsorship money.
Cockeyed drip.

Father,

*Apologies for not making it
back to pick up your ash-
es. For not allowing you to
know who I truly was. I'd
spent three years in hiding to
earn a real life. Your beloved
Amelia is not the tomboy the
world sees. She's not the pretty smile, nor the flight and
adrenaline lover. She is darkness incarnate. She is the devil
in disguise. She kills and does
not feel remorse.*

I tapped my pen against my pursed
lips. I could write anything and Edwin,
my dearest father, would never know.
I didn't continue, wondering if maybe
he'd been reading over my shoulder.
Not that I was ashamed; quite the op-

posite. I was proud to have shed the skin of the press pleaser.

Yawning, I closed my journal, and stood from my chair. I pulled the sheets down and climbed under them, laying my head on the pillow, my body on the bed. I closed my eyes, smiling.

"Hello, old friend. Welcome home," I said before falling asleep.

Two

I AWOKE FEELING REFRESHED — bright-eyed and bushy tailed, or something like a squirrel on coffee. My behavior wasn't quite resemblant, though I did have a spring in my step. I was happy to be back in the United States, instead of the island I'd been hiding on. I was sure it had a name, but I didn't speak the language so when locals I ran into said it, I had not a clue.

It was a pretty enough island...as pretty as one could be that's appearance was that of constant disheveled and torn. It had somehow escaped the touches of war, and still looked ravaged. People constantly running to and fro, ducking, even when planes were not overhead. It was as though the Koreans knew the island was there, but they were afraid of it.

I was not. I feared nothing, and proved that throughout my life. Not flying, not crashes—I'd been involved in many of those early in my pilot career, and then there was the last one. I'd purposely crashed that last time. I knew what I was doing. I *wanted* to crash. I needed a fresh start.

For three years I stayed there, keeping a low profile, only mingling with the villagers for food and shelter. I'd not needed to work, for there had been no monetary exchanges, but I did. I helped the women with their household chores and with their children. So many children, I began to despise the existence of them. My dark friend had started concocting plans to practice on them. I didn't—wouldn't—ever hurt a child. Their innocence is their beauty and simplicity.

I did not hone my skills on the island. I had spent time away from the public eye before prepping for this flight. My dark friend led me to dark alleys where people slept because they had nowhere and no one else. They were my first few, and certainly not my last.

I'd imagined killing George, but then people would suspect I was alive and I didn't want that. There had been plenty of men in my life I'd imagined killing, actually. That was all it would ever be, could ever be. At least for those I knew would be missed.

I'd cut my hair short and used the methods of dying the islanders used on my hair. It was raven black now. I was thinner than I'd ever been as an adult, though fit. All of this was in the name of remaining out of the eye of recognition. Only those who had known me would recognize as the gleam of my knife reflected in their eyes. Fred Noonan would be the first, now that I'd returned.

I needed a car, one that would look inconspicuous.

For days—before today—I sat on benches and watched the streets of

Glendale, watching and counting which one I'd seen most. Then, I followed one into a parking lot a few feet from where I'd been sitting. It was a Packard 120. A slick smile split my face, and I walked to the nearest car lot that had one for sale.

When I arrived, the salesmen brushed me off, thinking I was some regular woman, some housewife. I cleared my throat loudly, and a man who appeared to be around my age arched a brow at me.

"May I help you, ma'am?" He inquired.

"You may," I stated as I pointed to the silver Packard outside, "I'll take that one."

All heads turned to look at me, with more than a few gasps sounding.

"Uh, you want—"

"Yes," I interrupted. "I'd like to take it home now, please." I donned my most disarming smile, the same one I always gave the press. Still no one noticed who I was.

"Sure, um, how do you plan to pay?"

I pulled a handful of cash from my pocket.

"I believe this should cover it."

I set it down on the table in front of the confused man. He looked it over, and started counting.

"Great." His voice sounded more excited now. "Let's get the paperwork done and you'll be out of here in no time."

The voice in my head snorted as I sat down, disbelieving the term "no time."

An hour later, I was in the driver's seat of my brand new Packard 120 headed for Yuma, Arizona.

Three

I DIDN'T KNOW PRECISELY how many miles it was to Noonan's house, but I could read a map. That map read that it was somewhere around five hundred eighty miles to Yuma, though. That was enough for me. I'd stop somewhere to bed down once I grew tired enough.

For now, I was content to drive and enjoy the scenery. Not that driving beat the feeling of flying for me, but how was I supposed to fly? Imagine a woman walking into an airplane hangar. A woman who was not Amelia Earhart. The men would not appreciate that, let alone go along with her on a flight. Besides, I'd have to kill that man also. I wasn't interested in racking up too high a body count.

I had my list. If I needed to dispatch of others who got in my way, so be it. I simply didn't want more attention than necessary. I never had. GPP—as I called my husband George Palmer Putnam—wanted the attention and fame *for me*. It was vexatious, to say the least.

The radio played Judy Garland and Fred Astaire as I drove through the farmlands. The scenery was boring, crawling by at the posted speed limit of fifteen miles per hour. In contrast, my planes flew anywhere from one hundred seventy-six to one hundred ninety-five miles per hour. This felt like molasses in the winter.

I checked the speedometer to see how fast the new Packard would let me go—eighty-five miles per hour—then I put the pedal down and shifted into third gear. The two-door sedan was smooth in both shifting and ride, which was a much welcomed change from the Lockheed Model 10 Electra that bumped near-constantly, even at cruising altitudes.

I was contemplatively thoughtful on my drive. The world seemed to stand still, while I had not, could not. I had the ambition and drive to rival any man on this planet, and went after the things I wanted. Meanwhile, nothing in Glendale seemed to change, and driving on this road now, it appeared nothing here had changed either. Was no one wanting more from or with their lives?

I knew there was a war going on—I'd stolen an Asian plane from where I'd crashed, then another, a Howard DGA-15 from a military installation in Washington after the Asian plane had run out of fuel. Nothing and no one had seemed to change, though. I couldn't have been gone that long, could I?

Worse, was somehow, that drunkard Noonan, had escaped the Asian island without so much as a good-bye. I'd woken up one morning to find him gone. No note, he hadn't deemed it important to wake me...nothing. Fucking nogoodnik.

As I continued to drive, I mentally calculated how far I'd travel before needing to fill up this behemoth fuel tank and sleep for the night. Then, I checked the dashboard. It appeared I'd have to stop here shortly, which mildly annoyed yet contented me. I was growing hungry anyway, so it was as good a time as any to stop.

I drove another thirty minutes until I found a gas station and motel next to each other, where I filled the tank first. The attendant tried to fill it for me, but I wouldn't tolerate that, which was frowned upon in our society. After having seen how other countries lived, and how their women handled all they did, I was off-put by the socially accepted marginalizing of women in the United States.

When I was finished, I drove next door and into a parking space in front of the building. Before exiting the car, I checked my appearance in the rear-view mirror, verifying I did not look recognizable as me. Pleased, I opened the door and got out.

The bells on the door chimed as I opened it, and the older woman behind the counter greeted me warmly.

"Hello, Miss. How may I help you?"

"Hello," I replied with a smile, "One room please."

"Travelin' alone? That's improper for a lady," she commented, pulling a key from a box bearing the number "2" on the wall and setting it on the counter in front of me.

"I'm not afraid," I said, taking the key an nodding my thanks.

"That'll be three dollars, please."

I pulled the cash from my pocket and placed it in the woman's hand.

She nodded her thanks, then told me where my room was. She also told me where the bathroom was, as it was shared between all guests.

"You're the only one here tonight," she said with a wink.

I must have looked tense for her to have said that. I didn't mind shared bathrooms, though I didn't particularly enjoy them either.

I took the key, thanked her again, and walked to my room. It wasn't far from the office, about three doors down. I stuck the key in the doorknob and turned.

The room was clean, if dimly lit and drab. The single bed was clothed in crisp white sheets topped with a quilt. On the nightstand was a single lamp.

Walking deeper into the room, I noticed another table with a bible on top of it. I snorted, and lay down on the bed.

Staring at the ceiling, I spoke softly to the darkness inside me.

"Soon, I promise. Freddy will be ours. We know his mind is soaked in alcohol, which means he was stupid enough to go home to his wife, Mary. I do not want to kill her as well, though we will, you and me. Inevitably, she will get in the way, and make too much noise, as scared people do. Who do you think should die first?"

I stared, listening to my thoughts, until my eyelids grew heavy and fell asleep.

Four

I ROSE WITH THE sun, as its rays poked through the curtains. I hadn't a change of clothes, so I only brushed my teeth and rinsed my face in the bathroom before checking out.

As I drove off, the woman from behind the counter walked outside, presumably to check my room and clean it.

Back on the road, I found myself quickly bored. I wasn't even halfway to Yuma, though it was only a couple of miles difference of precisely halfway. The music and talk on the radio was also boring me. I needed to hear the roar of the airplane engine, not a sedan. I thrummed my fingers on the steering wheel for a different sound. I found myself wishing there was a drama on. At least that would have been entertaining.

I watched the farmland and emptiness go by, only half-listening to the songs and commercials on the radio. Somehow, I managed to lose track of time to the point I almost ran out of fuel.

Pulling into this station, I decided to let the attendant do his job and fill my tank for me. I needed something to help me stay awake, so I looked around, not seeing what I needed.

"Sir," I called, poking my head out of the window, "Would you happen to know where the closest diner is?"

He nodded, but didn't respond until he finished pumping.

"I sure do, ma'am. Which direction ya headin'?" He asked, taking his cap off and using it to wipe the sweat from his brow.

"East," I replied.

He pointed and gave me directions to the diner down the road. I thanked him and drove off.

I pulled into the diner's parking lot only a few minutes later, parking my silver beauty.

Inside, there were few people—two men at the counter, separated by two stools, and a couple in a corner booth. The couple had their heads down, presumably doing what kids these days did.

As took a seat at a booth near the door, a woman approached wearing a pink dress and dirty white waist apron. She set a menu down in front of me.

"Anything to drink?" She asked.

I looked up at her. She appeared no older than twenty, though she sounded much older. I assumed she was a smoker. Only that or alcoholism could have made her voice sound the way it did. Then, she sniffled. My assumptions had been proven wrong.

I smiled. "Yes, please. Coffee."

She nodded and walked away.

I perused the menu, quickly deciding on something light so I didn't get too sleepy on the rest of the drive. Not that I would have had issues; the closer I got to the kill, the more excited and awake I grew.

The waitress came back with my coffee and set it on the table in front of me. I nodded my thanks.

"Decide what you want?"

Again, I nodded. "I'll take the two eggs plate, please. Over-medium, with ham."

She wrote it down, took the menu, and walked back into the kitchen. I thought that odd. Usually, waitresses yelled to the cook in the back. I could only assume the woman's throat was too sore to yell.

I watched birds across the highway through the window—they were the most entertainment I'd experienced all day. Two sparrows chased a small flock of crows. There were almost no trees, so seeing sparrows confused me. Regardless, it gave me something to do. Seeing as I was in a diner, talking to myself was frowned upon.

We'll be kind when we arrive. Fred or Mary will invite us in, and we'll oblige. We'll talk about how we escaped the island and came home...

My thoughts were interrupted as the waitress returned with a plate bearing my breakfast. I thanked her and covered my lap with a napkin. Then, I seasoned my eggs with pepper before eating my breakfast, cutting the ham and dipping it in the beautifully cooked yolk, cutting the rest of the egg around the ham piece. I savored the mix of flavors, as I'd not tasted the simple meal in over two years.

I'd only learned I'd been gone over two years upon seeing a newspaper on my return. It had gobsmacked me. I'd known I'd been gone a long time, but to find out how long was a true shock.

I continued to fantasize while I ate my food, thinking of the ways I'd torture old Freddy. Mary wouldn't get too much, probably just a slit throat with her own kitchen knife. It wasn't she who'd lost track of where we were in the air. It wasn't she who'd been drunkenly navigating me and my plane for years, increasing the amount of drunk with each flight.

I could feel my face growing warmer with each thought. I glanced around to make sure no one had been watching me and breathed relief.

As I finished my breakfast, the waitress came over to ask if I wanted anything else while she refilled my coffee.

"Would you happen to have a way I can take a coffee with me?" I asked her.

"Sure do," she answered, and walked away again.

Wow! The advancements in only two years...

She returned holding an uncovered paper cup with handles. I frowned, confused as to how I would be able to drive with this.

"Thank you."

"Sure thing," she said, dropping the check on the table, "pay when you're ready."

I'd glanced at it as it fell and handed her the money, including tip.

"No change."

She simply nodded and walked away after placing the money in her apron pocket.

I stood, pausing to sip some coffee, hoping it would be enough to stop it from spilling all over me as I drove. I'd realized the only way to keep it still in any way would be to place it between my legs.

"What a fucking chore," I said to myself once I got into my car. "At least it's good coffee."

I was anxious and excited to keep moving, though I had not much clue where, exactly, I was.

The farther I drove, the more I'd started to look for signs to tell me where I was. Once I saw any, I could look at my map and gauge how many more miles I had to travel. Not that I knew *where* in Yuma Fred Noonan lived, but I was sure I could find a phone book to look him up, though.

Finally, I saw a sign for Anza, and pulled off to the side to check my map. I quickly realized I was still in California, though not for much longer. I had less than 200 miles to go. This also meant another stop for fuel. I shrugged and got back onto the roadway.

The rest of the drive to the next gas station was dull and uneventful. I hadn't even talked to my dark friend living inside me. Not that we had much to discuss, anyway.

After fueling up again, the time flew, as did the short distance. I arrived in Yuma not long after, and quickly spotted a diner where I could use the phone book to find Freddy. It was difficult to not run inside the building, given my level of excitement.

Inside, I scanned around and found the public telephone with the phone book set on a shelf underneath. The diner was busy, giving me ample cover so as to not be noticed too much.

Once at the phone, I grabbed the book and started flipping the pages, scanning for Noonan. I found him quickly and memorized the address before walking back out to my Packard. I picked up the map from the passenger seat, and found the street he lived on. Fortune must have been smiling on me because the street was only a few blocks away.

I pulled onto Freddy's street shortly after leaving the diner, and found his house in minutes. I grinned at myself in the rear view before exiting the car.

Five

THE PROPERTY WAS NICE enough. A beige colored house with a white front door, bare landscaping, and a black version of my car in the drive.

I walked to the front door, shielding my eyes from the midday sun. It was hot—not too hot, but hot enough that I'd started sweating a bit on my brow.

At the door, I took a deep breath to steady the rush of blood in my veins, then raised my fist to knock.

Mary appeared confused as she opened the door.

"Can I help you?"

"Hi, Mary. It's me. Amelia." I grinned broadly.

Her skin paled before her expression brightened, if falsely.

"Amelia! You must come in!" She opened the door wider, ushering me in as she called to Fred.

"Freddy! Fred! You will never believe who's here! Come join us!"

His response was faint and grumpy.

Good old Freddy. I smirked.

Mary beckoned me to follow her to the living room, motioning for me to have a seat on the couch. I smiled and nodded my appreciation as I sat.

"Thank you."

"Would you like some tea?" She asked.

"I would love some. Thank you, Mary." The false politeness was like knives inside my body.

As she rushed to the kitchen, Freddy came into the living room. When he saw me, he dropped the glass he was holding. It shattered all over the floor.

"Amelia?"

His face paled, body weakened as he slumped. I would not have been surprised if the man had soiled his shorts at that moment.

I stood, hand out to shake, warm smile on my face.

"Hey, Freddy. How have you been?"

"Uh, h-h-hi, Amelia. How...what...you—"

"I'll tell you everything. Let's sit."

Freddy inched to the chair across from me, hand out to feel for the arm, presumably to steady himself, and make sure he was sitting on the chair and not about to fall. He sat carefully, still making sure he wasn't going to fall.

Mary came back out carrying a tray bearing a glass pitcher of iced tea and three glasses. She set it on the coffee table and poured for all of us.

The perfect housewife, I sneered to myself. *Shame she won't need to be for much longer.*

I took a sip and smiled.

"Delicious."

Mary nodded.

"Thank you, Amelia. So, tell us, how did you make it back? I imagine it was an adventure... Like it was for Freddy."

The darkness inside me growled.

"Well," I said, setting my glass on the tray on the coffee table, "It sure was!"

I launched into the story of my "adventure" back to the states, not leaving anything out. When I was finished, Mary and Fred wore astonished looks.

"Wow, what a wild time you must have had! And how was the drive here? What made you come here?" Mary asked.

Freddy's face was still blanched. He knew why I was here. Maybe not entirely, but he knew he was the reason. He nodded in what appeared to be agreement with Mary.

"The drive was okay. And I'm here because I wanted to ask Freddy a question," I stated, trying not to sound threatening.

Freddy sat up straight.

"Ask me what?"

I let a tense moment pass between us, eyeing Freddy inquisitively.

"Why did you not say goodbye? Why did you leave without a single word or a note?"

Mary's head snapped to Freddy, clearly in shock. She had no clue why he would do such a thing. After all, he was her husband. And a drunkard.

He wasn't the worst human, though he wasn't the greatest either.

Freddy swallowed so hard I heard it. He stared at me, the abject fear evident in his eyes. He wasn't sure how to answer without upsetting me. Not that it mattered. He was already dead to me. And would be in reality soon enough.

"Well, I-uh-I..."

He looked from my eyes to the floor.

I didn't care how this question made him feel. I didn't care that he could not provide a satisfactory answer, even to himself or his wife. I did, however, know how to act. I smiled at him.

"Freddy," I said, "I'm not mad. I'm merely curious. I was worried when you were missing that day. And when you didn't return, my worry ceased, replaced by resigned sadness. I thought you'd died. So, I came to see Mary to offer condolences and comfort."

Fred looked at me, the relief clear. He let his breath out heavily, as though he'd been holding it, which I was sure he had been.

"Amelia, I'm so sorry. I should have said something. I was too preoccupied with getting off that island and coming home…"

I held up a hand.

"It's okay, Freddy."

He nodded.

Mary scowled at him, then looked to me.

"I'm terribly sorry Freddy left like that. If I'd have known—"

"You couldn't have done anything, anyway," I cut her off, still smiling. "It's okay, truly."

The three of us sat in silence, Freddy still fidgeting his gaze, unsure how he truly felt.

"May I use your restroom?" I asked.

"Of course!" Mary practically jumped from her seat. "It's down the hall. Second door on the left." She refilled all three glasses as I stood and walked out of the room.

On my way to the restroom, I made sure they were lost in conversation, and redirected to the kitchen. I began gently opening drawers, quietly rummaging for the perfect weapon.

Mary was still admonishing Freddy like he was a child who'd eaten sweets before supper.

I found the perfect knife in a drawer next to the stove—carefully closing after taking it so they wouldn't hear—and tucked it into my waistband. Then, I proceeded to the second door on the left down the hall. I didn't stay in there long. After all, they hadn't known I'd gone into the kitchen.

On my return, Freddy looked as glum as I'd ever seen him. I fought back a snicker.

Serves him right.

I did not sit back down immediately, instead putting my hands in my pockets, looking around the room.

"This is a great room," I complimented. A lie, of course. It was bright white, with a shelving unit made of metal and glass with knickknacks and one framed photo of Mary and Freddy on their wedding day on it. The walls held a mishmash of images—paintings?—that appeared as though a child made them.

"Would it be rude of me to ask for a tour?"

This time, Mary did jump from her seat, falling over herself.

"Of course not! Let's start in the kitchen."

Six

I LET MARY LEAD me through the kitchen she did not know I'd already been in. It was just off the living room. When we came out, Freddy was standing.

"I'll join you," he said, sounding like he was feeling better.

I smiled, as did Mary. I let the two of them guide me the rest of the way, not that there was much left to show me, but it felt right.

Mary pranced along, chattering excitedly as her animated hands fluttered and her voice crescendoed. Freddy started smiling as he watched Mary's animation. He was proud of what they'd built together, that was plain. Shame they would go down with it.

When Mary led us into the bedroom I made some noises that could have been understood as my liking the room. Them, I closed the door behind me.

Fred spun to face me, hearing the latch click, confused.

"What are you doing, Amelia?"

With a slow hand, I unveiled the blade tucked in my waistband, its steely surface dancing with reflected light. My face contorted into an ominous grin, revealing the depths of my darkness, both in reality and metaphorically.

Mary spun around, her mouth agape when she spotted the gleaming knife in my hand.

"Amelia? What's going on?"

"Shut up. Both of you." The words came out of my throat with such force and malice, they both dropped to sit onto the bed.

I played with the knife for a while, staring at it, admiring its simple beauty. Occasionally, I'd steal glances at Freddy and Mary, the horror etched into their faces. Each time I saw it, I laughed. I paced the room, terrorizing them more and more until I thought they might die of fear. Then I kneeled in front of them, knife still on display.

"My dear Freddy, you never truly knew me—no one did. I could have killed you on that island and not one person would have realized. They already thought we were dead! No search parties, nothing! DEAD!" I paused to take a few breaths and calm down. My voice was lower now, more feral and dark. "Hell, even GPP moved on. With life insurance money he'd gotten from declaring *me* dead."

Mary's expression showed her sadness and regret at knowing this had happened.

I nodded.

"Of course you knew, Mary, it must have been all over the papery—every headline!—for weeks," I chided.

She started crying and nodding.

"It was," she sobbed, "I wish I'd known!"

Faster than a bolt of lightning, I snapped the knife to her neck.

"Shut. Your. Fucking. Mouth. There was nothing—would never be anything—you could do to change things. To change anything! All you could have done was whine at people and raise a fuss, nothing more. Less? Sure, there's always less people can do. Including you. Hell, I'd be willing to bet you thought Freddy was dead and tried to have him pronounced so that you could collect on his life insurance policy," I growled, gently caressing her neck with the knife, my face inches from hers.

She sobbed harder, her chest and shoulders heaving, her breath coming out in gasps.

"Oh, stop, you're such drama queen. No one cares. Especially not me." I stopped and looked her straight in the eyes. "You're as bad as he is." I motioned to Freddy with the knife tip.

Mary started screaming. Whether it was at Freddy or for help, I couldn't be certain, nor did I care. I snapped the blade back up against her throat, drawing a thin line of blood.

"Keep screaming," I taunted, "You'll make your death that much more painful."

I grinned, similar to how I imagined the Cheshire Cat did. Mary recoiled, horrified.

"See, your *Freddy*, has a habit of being disappointing. Disappointment breeds distrust, frustration, and anger." I said, the venom dripping from my words. "But for me, it's not the anger thing that actually gets to me. It's the distrust. See—" I tipped the knife point to my chin and scratched "—as a navigator, he's supposed to be able to be trusted... With someone's life."

I cackled.

"What a sham he is. Anyway, Mary, I don't *want* to kill you, but you're a witness who can identify me, so... I'm sorry."

I sliced in one swift motion, my wrist flicking, hoping she didn't feel too much pain and that whatever pain she did feel didn't last too long. Within minutes, she was gone. Pale on the bed, blood soaking the duvet, her eyes pointed toward the ceiling. Her face was contorted in what I could only assume was a last attempt at a scream.

Freddy vomited. I laughed.

"Aw, the alcoholic can't handle a little bit of blood? Interesting, since we killed animals to SURVIVE!" I screamed at him.

He shuddered as he countered.

"No, A-Amelia. Y-y-you killed the animals. I stayed back. Never could handle the thought of blood, let alone the sight of it." He hung his head, as if he was less of a man.

My laugh erupted from my belly as I threw my head back.

"Pussy," I teased. "You're as bad as a woman."

I paced in front of him, letting him wonder what I'd do next. When I'd slit his throat. Little did he know, I was planning a few measures of torture before giving him the sweet mercy of death.

For the next few minutes, Freddy stuttered, frantically trying to get words out of his mouth at all. His face would twist and contort as though he was fighting internal monologue of what he could—or should—say to ease the situation he found himself in. It was clear, however, there was nothing he could say, and he'd realized that.

I squatted in front of him, knife tip to my pursed lips. I was thinking what I wanted to start with. Then, I grinned, and slashed at the back of his left ankle.

Freddy let out a howl of pain, bringing his injured leg up to his chest, gripping the now-severed tendons as though he could magically reverse what I'd just done.

I let him cry and rock back and forth for a little while, staring at the blood on the knife. So much blood. It made my darkness happy to see him in pain like this; the blood made me happy.

Freddy calmed down to a sort of grunting, though he still rocked. It was the perfect moment to strike again.

I slashed at his right ankle in the same area. I felt the ligaments and tendons cleanly sever, the major one popping, and maliciously grinned.

This time, he didn't bother to pull his leg up. He did jerk a bit like he was going to, but just...gave up.

I sprung to a standing position.

"What the *fuck* is wrong with you? You're giving up? No fight?" I spat. "Fucking worthless... I don't know what Mary ever saw in you. You're no man, you're a child in a man's body. You have no remorse, no care for anyone but yourself, and no balls! What a waste!"

Now, I was truly angry. What kind of person didn't try to fight back? Particularly after having just one achilles severed? That *had* to be excruciating! Yet, here was this "man," sitting on the bed, rocking while grasping that first severed major tendon. The blood was everywhere, and Freddy was fading. I'd have to speed this up if I wanted him to feel the rest of the pain I wanted to inflict.

I thought for a second and realized I'd started on the wrong extremity. I should have started with ripping his fingernails out, *then* the ankles. I heaved an annoyed sigh and bent over, knife blade to his throat.

"Goodbye, Freddy. You really did lose yourself inside those bottles. I might miss the person you were—" I cocked my head to one side then straightened it "—probably not."

I slit his throat to be sure he couldn't cry out for help even though I knew he'd bleed out from both ankles in the next few minutes. I'd have to try the fingernail thing on someone else.

Seven

LEANING OVER FREDDY'S AND Mary's dead bodies, I smiled one last time, wishing I had a camera so I could relive the memory. I'd settle for the pictures in my head.

Before leaving the room, I wiped the blade on Freddy's shirt to clean it, then tucked it back into the waist of my pants. I strode down the hall and back into the living room, where I finished my glass of iced tea, used the bathroom one last time, and left.

Outside, the sun was setting. It was a beautiful sight. I'd missed these while on the island. Not to say those sunsets weren't beautiful in their own right, but something about being back in the States made me feel...free.

Back in my Packard, I laughed as I started it up, and looked at the map, choosing my final destination. I knew it would take about a week to get there. I wasn't sure how precisely many miles, but I approximated almost 3,000. Factoring in how often I would need to stop to refuel the car and eat, sleep, I was looking at a long, dull drive. Maybe on the road, I'd perfect my torture skills. I grinned in the rear view and set out for the interstate.

The open road made me miss the sky. Planes were much faster, needed to stop less for fuel. Though, the skies were much more unpredictable. Winds could change everything, and that was what I enjoyed the most. It was a challenge. Driving on empty roads, with nothing around me but farmland and cows was less satisfying. However, it was relaxing. I was still riding the high from killing Freddy and Mary, so it was the most perfect way to feel it; to enjoy it.

I was still high when I glanced down at the fuel gauge, letting out a grumble of displeasure.

"Definitely not a plane," I muttered, keeping an eye out for a gas station.

I found one a few miles away and refueled, grabbing a soda pop from the machine while the attendant cleaned the windows after pumping. I paid him, and drove off.

The scenario repeated one more time before I decided to find a motel and bed down for the night. Once in my room, I opened my journal that I kept in my glove box. I re-read the letter I'd penned to my father, Edwin. I teared up a little as I'd never gotten to say good-bye. I missed the man I knew him to be.

I turned the page and wrote him another letter. It was all I could do to have a conversation with him, albeit a short one.

I miss you, father.

Love,
Amelia

I carefully placed the ribbon between the pages and closed the book before standing and walking the five feet from the desk to the bed and lay down. Staring at the ceiling, as I had a habit of doing, I thought about choosing my next victim. I wondered what city or town I'd be in and what type of person they'd be.

I decided a large town or city would be best to avoid detection and prying eyes. Smaller towns held the likeliness that everyone knew each other and gossip would spread like wildfire. Gossip triggered investigations. Those who had known I was alive were now dead by my hands. It would continue that way.

I like the idea of it being a man. After all, we're headed for George Palmer Putnam and his new wife, Jean-Marie Cosigny James, next.

I nodded my head.

"I concur. Though men have lower thresholds for physical pain than women," I mused. "Regardless, it would still be fun. And it gives me the ability to practice what I'll be doing to GPP. His wife is just another witness to me. I don't know her; she means nothing to me." I thought for a few moments. "Yes, we'll pick a random man in Chicago. That is a large enough city. It should be a simple thing to find a man there."

With that, I smiled, finally relaxed enough to close my eyes and fall asleep.

I awoke the next morning feeling rejuvenated now that I had my next major destination—and torture subject—mapped out in my mind. I brushed my teeth, picked up my journal, and checked out.

I contemplated they type of man I'd ultimately choose while I drove. I was sure I'd have a few more days' drive ahead of me before I could even consider finding that man. I also thought about how long I'd stay in Chicago *before* the kill. Staying longer than two days would be boring, however, so I'd decided on that as a top end limit.

I'd avoid the south side so as not to irritate the mob by accidentally choosing one of theirs. I'd need a busy bar, one where for as many witnesses, there would be less to speak up about seeing a man leave with a woman. After all, it was a common practice the world around, growing more common the further into the future we traveled.

By the time I needed to refuel, the sun was already high in the sky. This time, the gas station was conveniently located right next to a diner. I fueled up and drove the several yards to a parking space in the diner's lot.

Inside, the air conditioning was blasting. It felt nice—the Midwest was dry and hot. Not as hot as Southern California or Yuma, but still warm enough to need the cooler air indoors.

I nodded to the woman behind the counter as she looked up at me, picked up a newspaper, and sat in a booth toward the end. I'd just started reading the front page when she walked up.

"What can I get ya?" She inquired.

"Coffee, please," I responded, picking up the menu from the table. "May I have a few minutes to peruse?"

She nodded. "I'll get your coffee," she said before walking away.

It took me no more than thirty seconds to scan and decide what I was going to order. Another thirty or so seconds later, the waitress returned, setting the coffee down in front of me. She pulled out a notepad and pen from her waist apron.

"What'll it be?"

"Burger, well done. Tomato on the side, please. May I also have an extra pickle?"

She nodded, writing my order down.

"Oh, and a Coke, please."

She nodded again and took the menu, leaving me to my newspaper.

The only real thing of interest to me was where I actually was. Apparently, I was somewhere in Phoenix, Arizona. This didn't feel like a big city. Perhaps, I was on the outskirts. I made a face, curtly nodded my head to one side. No matter.

I continued to read the newspaper, stories of Germany occupying Czech territory and Austria being annexed to Germany. Hitler was getting more and more brazen. I almost commended him for it. Almost.

While I *was* a killer, I did not condone killing people simply because of who people were.

Fucking dictators. They take what they want, kill whomever they want, and for what?

The waitress returned with my food and Coke, pulling me from the verge of anger.

"Thank you."

She only nodded and walked away.

I picked up a pickle spear and bit into it, still thinking.

Men... The horrors they were capable of. If only they realized women were just as dangerous...

Eight

I WATCHED AROUND THE diner as I ate. Children played in the walkway while the parents seemed oblivious. Frustration grew inside me.

Of course, I had some level of empathy, but not enough to be truly affected. Instead, I felt for the children who would surely receive a whooping for acting out in public.

Nevertheless, I continued contemplating my next kill. I'd lure the man out of the bar, having him take me back to his place. Ideally, he'd be a single man who lived alone. I'd need a few more supplies, particularly pliers and maybe a bucket for warm water. I held no illusions about the difficulty of pulling out fingernails.

My meal was as satisfying as my progression of plans. I was finishing my fries when the waitress returned one last time to drop my check on the table.

"You can pay when you're ready," she stated before walking away again.

I nodded and smiled, still chewing, knowing how rude it would be to speak with my mouth full.

A few minutes later, I stood, paid, and left. I was anxious to get back on the road, but not so much, as the dread of how many more stops I'd have to make started to set in.

Inside my car, I opened the glove box, admiring the knife I'd taken from the Noonan house after killing them with it. It would be what I used to kill my next, along with George and Jean-Marie. Though, it might be more *meaningful* if I used one of theirs. I shook that thought from my head. There was a good chance it wouldn't matter much what I used, so long as I killed the one who helped me fully realize what I was. Slowly, so he could appreciate the truth.

I'd always thought there was something wrong with me. I knew I was different. I enjoyed killing things as a child. Even as I grew up, I still enjoyed killing things. Then, I'd gotten into flying airplanes. For me, the adrenaline rush was similar from the two activities.

Two stops for fuel, and another motel room later, I was back at a desk with my journal open in front of me. I read the words I'd written over the previous weeks, reliving the kills of Freddy and Mary in my mind at the same time. I also read the words I'd written to my father, knowing the end then. My end.

Once in bed, I stared at the ceiling, as was my ritual before falling asleep.

You cannot.

"But I can. And I will."

What's the point of it?

"To be together again."

No. I won't allow it.

"Like you have a choice."

I smirked in spite of the darkness inside me—in spite of myself. After all, it was myself I was conversing with.

Closing my eyes, my darkness started to speak again, instead choosing to itself.

The next morning was just like the rest. I woke, brushed my teeth, grabbed my journal, and checked out. This morning, however, I decided to take my time and at least *try* to enjoy it, choosing to stop at the next diner I found for breakfast.

Forty minutes later, I exited, appalling paper cup filled to the brim with coffee, in hand.

"Why are these cups so fucking terrible?" I complained, carefully lowering myself into the driver's seat.

Before starting the car, I sipped the piping hot, black liquid before carefully setting it between my legs.

"There has got to be a better way to do this."

It dawned on me then. I could find a store to purchase something on my way. There *had* to be something. I racked my brain and recalled seeing something at the base in Washington I'd stolen the plane from. It was cylindrical, and the lid could be used as a cup. I'd find one somehow. Maybe there was something similar for civilians.

It didn't take long for me to finish the coffee as I drove, and my annoyance wore off. The scenery changed, too. More trees, less brownish-yellow emptiness.

During my next fuel stop, I asked where I was.

"Adrian, Texas, ma'am," the man said with a drawl.

"What's there to do in the area?" I asked. "I'm driving cross-country and would love to see some sights instead of what I have been seeing."

He paused a moment, pondering my question.

"Well, there's a canyon in Amarilla," he replied. "Which direction you headed, anyway?"

"East," I answered, thinking about what a relaxing time a canyon would be. "Amarillo you said?"

I pulled my map off the passenger seat, opening and scanning for Amarillo. I found it just as the man spoke again.

"Yes, ma'am. It's about fifty or so miles east."

"Perfect, thank you."

I handed him the money for the fuel and got back on the highway, Amarillo bound.

When I arrived, I stopped into the first open business I saw, a pharmacy, to ask directions to the nearest chain store. The man behind the counter gave them happily. I thanked him and left.

Once in the store, I found precisely what I was looking for and more. It was a lunch "kit" consisting of a lunch pail and the exact replica of those cylindrical containers with the cup as a lid. As I was paying for my items, I asked the cashier how to get to the canyon.

Nine

THE SHRUBBERY AROUND THE sign indicating I was approaching Palo Duro Canyon State Park was a vibrant green, standing out vividly against the otherwise dull and uninspiring landscape. I sighed, feeling somewhat elated to be doing something different, as I turned onto the road that would take me into the park.

What the fuck are you doing?

"Hell if I know. I just needed a change. Something to kill some time, I guess."

Bullshit. You needed time to think. Are you getting soft on me?

"No! And correct. We still have plenty of time. It's not like we need to kill again right this minute," I huffed at myself.

Are you certain of that?

The way my darkness asked that question, the tone of it, was... What? What was it? Why was I so bothered by it? This assuredly was not the first time it had spoken to me this way. It certainly wouldn't be the last, either. Or would it?

As I crept along the road looking for a decent parking spot, I took in the views around me. It was breathtaking. I could not begin to imagine what the canyon itself looked like, but the excitement in me was growing.

I found a parking space and walked toward the canyon's edge. A small group stood there, murmuring in awe and inspiration. Their excitement sparked my hopes. I was in the right place. This was where I needed to be.

When I reached the edge, careful to avoid the group so as not to be recognized, I froze. The sight before me took my breath away. It was the most awe inspiring thing I'd ever seen on land. If I'd been in love with the freedom of being in the sky, this was a new form of love. One of absolute wonderment and peace.

Astounded, I stood there, paralyzed by the awe I felt. Even my darkness was silent. She had no comments, negative or positive, as though even she was exhilarated. Palo Duro truly was where we needed to be at this moment.

I do not know how long we stood there before moving to walk along the edge, but we did. And I took in as much of the sights as I could while making sure I stayed away from the edge. After all, I had things to do and people to kill before I would accept death.

What if we killed someone here? We could use them as practice?

"No," I muttered quietly so no one close would hear, "That's why we're stopping in Chicago for a few days."

Mhm.

I snorted, and kept walking, looking into the canyon as I did. The sun had begun its descent, casting shadows that I got lost in. Below, the nature that bloomed continued to keep me in awe.

There were so many colors, sprawled throughout; it was a scene I didn't think possible before now. There was a map posted a few feet away from where I was, so I walked up to it, wanting to know more about this place.

Palo Duro Canyon was one hundred twenty miles long. I didn't plan to walk the whole thing. I could have, but it would take many days longer than I was willing to spend.

I did 'hike' a few miles in before deciding to turn around and and head back to my car for the night. I'd decided I wanted to come back tomorrow, and maybe the next day, for no other reason than to absorb the peace and beauty before I set back out on my bloody, torturous journey.

The people in my mind's eye had no idea what was about to befall them, and I did not feel the least bit bad about it. GPP tried to control me, and had succeeded, for the most part. His wife, Jean-Marie, was merely a witness. As for the casual kill in Chicago, well, he was unaware of me or my plans, so that mattered not, as well. He was to be practice.

There were plenty of motels and such nearby, so I chose the one with the least amount of vehicles in the lot. I paid cash, and went to my room. This one had a private bathroom, which was a welcome change. I hadn't had one yet on this trip, so I was grateful. Evading people who knew who I was was, after all, my largest challenge.

After I'd taken a shower, I sat at the desk and wrote in my journal. This time, however, it wasn't a letter to Edwin. It was my thoughts and feelings. Not that I really *had* feelings anymore. After all I'd been through—Amy and Muriel had all but forsaken me for being different, GPP had controlled me so I could please him, the wreck on that island—I had decided to shut them out. People were horrifying creatures.

The words poured out of me as though my darkness had been the one writing them. Words like 'death,' ending it,' and others clouded the page. To be concise, they were not words of anger or hatred; they were words describing the justice I'd take.

The last I knew, Amy and Muriel were still alive. I couldn't go after them because that would out me. Aside from that fact, I simply did not want to. Everyone else? I wanted to.

Amy was the start of who, nay *what*, I was. That morsel of truth hadn't escaped me. I had a plan, and I was going to stick to it. She was not involved.

She should be, the cunt.

"Correct, but she's not part of the plan. And I have no desire to go to jail. We both know that if I killed her, too, the cops would suspect a common link between her and George. No," I responded.

Hmph.

I almost heard her crossing her arms over her chest, and snickered.

The happy Amelia the world saw never truly existed. She was but a show. One I'd continue to put on for as long as I needed to.

Ten

MURDER WAS ON MY mind as I opened my eyes. I stared at the ceiling, the sunlight playing upon it. The moonlight hadn't been when I'd fallen asleep, but this was not anything new to me.

My darkness was my friend, confidante, and also enemy. She was everything I was not on the outside, everything I should have openly been, however glad I was not. She was angry for me— for the woman I was *forced* to be.

This morning, like many others, she'd let me know that in no uncertain terms. The days I woke up with murder on my mind were simply her asserting her dominance, or maybe reminding me she existed. Either way, I had always known she was there. If it hadn't been to her liking, oh well.

I brushed my teeth, and read my journal. I usually didn't remember what I'd written the night before, and the refreshers helped me go about my days. It was something about the mere knowing of how I'd fully felt and thought the night before that kept me on a flatter road, having more stability than the one I knew I was on. This one would lead me to my ultimate destination.

I decided I wanted to take a shower. The dilemma was clean clothes. That was something I hadn't even considered needing. Why would I have? My sole concerns when I left Glendale were Fred Noonan and George Palmer Putnam. Anything that didn't involve either of them was irrelevant.

But now? Now, that rang untrue. Now, I wanted a shower and could take one. Now, I wanted fresh, clean clothes and I could have them. Now...

I sat upright, flinging the the journal onto the bed, practically tossing it. I donned my worn clothes and headed out to the registration desk.

Once there, I informed the male clerk that I intended to stay another night. He nodded, told me how much it would cost, and I paid him.

I left the office and got into my car, now knowing where some things were around town. I went to the store I'd been in for the lunch kit, and picked out some more feminine-style clothing, as well as work-style clothing. After all, this was not just a sight-seeing trip.

I went back to my room, took a bath, and put on the work-style clothing I'd purchased. I wanted to take a small hike or walk through the canyon and the dress wouldn't do it.

Thirty minutes later, I was exiting my car in the Palo Duro Canyon parking lot I was in the day prior. I shielded my eyes, the sun blinding me even though I had aviator sunglasses on. The colors were just as blinding in the bright light of day. It was absolutely stunning.

The Palo Duro Canyon stretched before me, a vast and rugged expanse carved by the relentless forces of nature. Towering sandstone cliffs, tinged with hues of orange and red, rose majestically from the canyon floor, casting long shadows that danced across the landscape as the sun arched overhead. The vibrant colors and intricate patterns etched into the rock formations were a testament to the canyon's rich geological history.

As I descended into the canyon's depths, the world seemed to transform around me. The narrow trail wound through a labyrinth of rock formations, each one more awe-inspiring than the last. Juniper and mesquite trees dotted the canyon floor, their twisted branches reaching towards the sky, while the occasional splash of wildflowers added a burst of color to the earthy tones that surrounded me.

The canyon's grandeur was complemented by the subtle sounds of nature that echoed through the vast expanse. The gentle trickle of a stream, the call of a distant canyon wren, and the whisper of the wind through the juniper trees created a symphony that reminded me of the canyon's timeless beauty and serenity.

I wasn't sure exactly how long the canyon had been here, but it was developed by the Civilian Conservation Corps from 1933 to 1937. So, it was about as new as I was to coming back to the United States. However, I knew the canyon formed much farther back in time than that. It *felt* a million years old.

I shivered.

I feel its energy. It's definitely ancient.

"Thanks for your two cents. You're feeling energy now?" I shook my head.

Always have. You were just too busy to notice.

I scoffed as I kept walking.

The yawning chasm before me seemed to stretch into eternity, its carved crimson walls towering impossibly high above. With each stride, the awe-inspiring canyon unveiled newfound depths of grandeur that left me breathless. The raw power of nature's artistry was almost too much to comprehend as I drank in the kaleidoscope of burnt oranges, deep reds, and blazing ambers.

Entranced, I pressed onward, losing all sense of fatigue or thirst. But soon the merciless desert sun began its descent, casting long shadows that crept across the canyon floor. I knew I had ventured too far and must turn back before nightfall trapped me in this majestic yet unforgiving abyss. As much as it pained me, I stole one last glance at the sublime landscape before reluctantly retracing my steps, knowing I would never return.

Back at my car, I paused to catch my breath for a few moments before getting back behind the wheel.

As I turned out onto the highway, headed back to the motel, the sun was setting. Through the glare in my rear view, the red and blue flashing lights came up fast.

Eleven

I PULLED OVER ONTO the dirt shoulder, both hands on the wheel. I waited for what felt like too long, but was only a few seconds.

The police car sped by me, and, with an audible "whoosh," I let out the air in my lungs I was unaware I was holding. I shifted into gear, and got back on the road.

Back in my motel room, I journaled about the wonder and beauty I experienced in the canyon:

I may be a killer, heartless sometimes, but that does not mean that I am incapable of appreciating such grounding and awe-inspiring experiences.

I paused, staring at the wall, tapping the pen against my lips. I was reliving the scenery, the vivid colors popping against the backdrop of neutral tones. The greens, blues, and purples exploded in my vision, giving me a new appreciation for nature.

When I came back to, I continued to write, detailing in another letter to Edwin what I'd seen today. I'd written him a lot of letters in this journal, knowing he'd never be able to read them. They were simply my way of talking to him.

Drawing the blanket down and climbing into bed after finishing this latest letter, I stared at the ceiling, as always. I found it was the easiest way for me to clear my mind, silence my darkness, and fall asleep. Usually, she spoke up about one thing or another, and tonight was no exception.

We should keep moving instead of staying another night.

"Why? There is no rush," I argued.

Because people may start to notice us here. Why don't we stay longer in Chicago, instead? It's a big city, and I'm sure there are plenty of places for us to stay. What I mean to say is, we can stay at a different place each night or every couple of nights or something.

I mulled that over for a few moments.

"I'll sleep on it, but I think you have a point."

With that, I closed my eyes.

The next morning, I bathed and donned the more feminine clothing I'd purchased. It was uncomfortable, as I was more used to what was now referred to as "women's work wear," or in my specific case, aviation gear.

The dress came down to the middle of my calf. It was light blue with no pattern or design; simplicity was key to not standing out. I'd need to purchase more clothing, though I'd do so in Chicago where there were more stores.

The male clerk behind the counter gave me a look and a low whistle when I went to check out. I rolled my eyes, fighting not to scoff at him. Why did men act that way, anyway? Did they think it turned us on? Fucking morons. I pasted on a painful smile, thanked him, and went on my way.

The drive was once again uneventful and dull. I stopped for coffee every time I stopped for fuel. It was all I could do to keep my eyes open, even though I was nowhere close to tired. I drove for about eight hours before deciding to find another motel room with a private bathroom to stay the night.

At least this clerk was a woman, also wearing a pale blue dress, though hers bore a flower design. She nodded at me, a compliment. I returned the gesture, though with words.

"Your dress is very pretty," I said, "Where did you find it? I'd love to have one also."

She gave me the name of the store and directions.

"They're closed now, but open at 10 am tomorrow."

"Thank you! I'll head over after I check out."

I took my room key, and left. On the wall outside the office was a map of Missouri. I was in Sullivan, about an hour and a half southwest of St. Louis. Also, approximately four and a half hours from Chicago.

In my room, I began my nightly ritual, sitting at the desk with my journal and pen. Some thoughts and a letter to

Edwin later, I was in bed staring at the ceiling again.

You know...

I was slightly annoyed that she'd trailed off like that.

"What?"

We could stay three or four days in Chicago. We're making great time.

"We could. It's not like I have a set date to kill George."

Do you feel bad we have to kill Jean-Marie?

"No. Witnesses are bad, remember?"

She hummed an agreement.

I liked that woman's dress, too. Maybe we should get it in other colors, if they have it?

"Yes. Yes, we should. I like that idea," I agreed. "Though, I'm not the most comfortable in dresses. Especially since George forced me to wear them. It's not that I never knew my place as a woman. I simply resented it."

As did I, Amelia. As did I. Do you think that's where I came from?

I chuckled.

"No. I believe we were born, not made."

With that, I closed my eyes.

Twelve

After checking out, I held to my plan of buying more dresses and skirts. Inside the store the clerk had recommended, I found a metaphorical treasure trove. Their ladies' section held more than I'd seen in quite some time. Sure, I'd been to major department stores with GPP, but I'd never seen the size of this section outside one of those.

Easily finding the dress the motel clerk had on, I selected that one, and a few others in my size. I also chose a couple of skirts and pretty blouses—all clothes I expected and had seen on "normal" women. I was one of "them." On the outside, at least.

The woman at the cash register looked at me, practically gaping.

"Wow! You look like a woman on a mission!"

If you only knew.

"Mission accomplished, I'd say," I responded with a grin.

She nodded, her excitement plain as day. Then she chatted happily while she rang me up and used hanging bags on all of my garments. When she told me the total, she flinched. I did not. I paid, thanked her, took my new clothes, and left.

There was no way to hang everything inside my car, so I laid it down on the back seat. If it came to it, I'd have to trash anything that got too wrinkled. I needed to look perfectly ladylike and didn't have time to wait for dry cleaning.

On the road once more, I realized drinking coffee while driving *and* wearing a dress was cumbersome at best. It was awkward, and less than desirable. At least I had my bottle so it didn't spill.

Four hours should go by quickly, even with the two or three fuel stops I'd need to make. I figured on three, just so I could drive around the city to decide where I'd spend the first two nights. Also, to check out what was located where - bars, diners, coffee shops, jazz clubs... Did Chicago even have jazz clubs? Only one way to find out.

This leg of the trip was much more lively looking. It was less barren, more green and sort of homely. What I meant by that was there were more homes, less farms and open land. It was nice to be in an area where there were more people.

Which also made me uneasy. I'd be more difficult to spot, yet easier. More people meant more to blend in with, and more to potentially recognize me. At least the pickle I'd find myself in would be delicious. As would our next kill.

I started daydreaming about the kind of man I'd choose to play with. He'd be a little taller than me, dark hair, with goofy grin in a boyish sort of way. It was almost as though I could see him in my mind. Not that I expected my imagination to be reality. I shrugged, finished my coffee, and checked the fuel gauge. Half a tank left, which really meant a quarter of a tank before I had to fill up again. Even with planes, I always tried not to let the gauge hit the "E" line.

Soon after, I did stop for fuel, was expeditiously hit on by the attendant, and got back on the road after politely declining. Both me and my darkness growled. We despised men like that.

We should have killed him, too.

"No," I replied flatly, "I'm not trying to leave a treasure map of bodies. Those we kill have already been selected. With the exception of the torture practice."

The darkness inside snickered.

The torture practice.

I grinned, looking for a diner or something. My stomach was making loud noises and there was no way I was going to stay anywhere near that grease ball.

I found a cute diner a few miles up the road and pulled in. The outside looked weathered and faded, but clean, with a hand-painted sign proclaiming "Millie's Home Cookin'." That sounded promising.

Inside was a surprisingly warm and inviting scene. Ash wood paneling covered the walls, complemented by ruby red vinyl booths and stools along a U-shaped counter. The smell of bacon, coffee, and burgers filled the air. Only a few other customers were scattered around, leaving me to pick any available seat I wanted.

I chose a booth against the back wall, sliding across the cracked vinyl. It snagged a bit of the fabric of my dress, but when I pulled it free, there was no damage. Crisis averted.

An older woman with a warm smile and a coffee pot immediately materialized at my side.

"Coffee, hon?" She asked in a smoker's raspy voice.

I nodded. "Please, black is fine."

She filled my cup, and pulled a pen and pad from her apron pocket. "Ya know what ya want or need a minute?"

"I'll have the All-American Cheeseburger with onion rings instead of fries, please," I replied.

"Sure thing, sugar."

"Perfect, thank you."

The waitress scribbled my order and headed back behind the counter. I took a sip of the steaming coffee, pleased at its rich flavor. This wasn't a bad place for a lunch break.

As I waited for my food, my mind inevitably wandered back to my upcoming time in Chicago. I was looking forward to a bit of anonymity in the big city before having to deal with George and his new wife, Jean-Marie. The practice kill would let me refine my torturing methods on a fresh victim, without any emotional attachment.

A hint of unease flickered through me at the thought. Not guilt exactly, but a small twinge of something. Doubts? Trepidation? Whatever it was, I quickly shoved it away. I was who I was—a killer living out her true nature. No use questioning it now after going this far down the path. I'd never questioned it before, so why start now, anyway?

At least you've learned that.

I snorted.

The waitress reappeared, shattering my momentary discourse as she slid a plate piled high in front of me.

"There ya go, sugar. Anything else I can getcha?"

I shook my head and picked up my fork. "This looks wonderful, thank you."

She patted my shoulder with a grand-motherly smile. "You just let me know if you need anythin' else."

I dug into the the onion rings first, then picked up the giant burger with both hands, finding each bite more delicious than the last. I learned that I'd need to cut the monstrosity in half the second I'd taken my third bite. Simple food like this pleased my darkness, for she appreciated the same simplicities I did.

Small-town places like this are under-rated. There's such warmth and comfort here. Something we're not used to.

I had to agree. The diner put me at ease in its cozy, unpretentious way. A bit of country charm along the highway. I made a mental note to seek out diners like this one in my travels. Though I'd never publicly admit it, they provided a kind of tranquility to balance the storm always raging inside me.

All too soon, I'd cleaned my plate. I lingered just a few more minutes over the last sips of coffee before reluctantly rising and making my way to the register to pay. The matronly woman manning the counter gave me another grandmotherly smile.

"You have yourself a nice day now, you hear?" She said warmly.

I couldn't help but return her smile. "I will, thank you...Millie, was it?"

She laughed, the sound full of kindness. "That'd be me, sugar. You take care of yourself out there."

With a final wave, I pushed through the diner's doors and back out into the mild spring day. The quaint stop had lifted my spirits more than I would have expected. I took a deep, steadying breath and climbed back into my car to continue the journey, refreshed in both body and mind.

Since when do you care about people's names?

"Since shut the fuck up," I admonished when we were back on the road.

Within a couple of hours, the first Chicago suburbs began appearing along the highway.

Thirteen

The urban sprawl grew thicker and thicker as I drove, the landscape transitioning from open fields to tightly packed houses to towering office buildings and condos.

Traffic also steadily increased until I was caught in a snarling, honking gridlock. I gripped the steering wheel tightly, the roar of engines and blaring horns grating on my nerves. So much for the tranquility from the diner wearing off anytime soon.

Calm down. This is just the outskirts. The city itself can't be much farther. Besides, what good would it do either of us if we flipped out?

I took a deep, cleansing breath and willed myself to relax. She was. unfortunately, right. I would be free of this soon if I could just get into the heart of Chicago proper. The thought of getting lost alone in its crowded streets and anonymity filled me with a bit of excitement that helped override the frustration.

At last, I broke free from the knot of vehicles to find myself in the bustling downtown area. Soaring skyscrapers crowded all around, their steel and glass facades glittering in the midday sun. A kaleidoscope of signs, awnings, and banners adorned the streets in a anarchy of colors and lights that dazzled the eye.

I slowly cruised along, eyeing the scenery like tourist would. Technically, I was one this time around. The sheer size and scale of the city was almost a breath of fresh air after traversing the country's vast, dull open spaces for so long. If a place like this didn't offer the anonymity I needed, nowhere would.

Focus, Amelia. We need to find a place to stay first before we get distracted by the things we'll soon be doing.

"Buzz kill," I muttered.

Giving myself a mental shake, I nodded and began scanning for hotels. I quickly realized that finding a room might be a little trickier than I'd anticipated in this crowded metropolis. Most of the accommodations appeared to be upscale hotels. I had the money, and it wasn't like I'd really be spending it on much else.

I must have circled the downtown area half a dozen times, growing increasingly frustrated by the overwhelming amount of choices, before I finally threw my hands up and picked one at random.

The lobby inside was unlike anything I'd ever seen before. Gigantic crystal-adorned chandeliers decorated the vaulted ceiling. Marble floors that my heels clicked on as I walked to the counter. There was even a lounge just off the lobby playing jazz music. I smiled.

"Hello! Can I get a room for a couple of nights? Maybe three?" I asked the man behind the counter.

He gave me a judgmental once-over, making no effort to hide his ogling my figure in the knee-length floral print dress I'd picked up earlier. Typical. I fought the urge to roll my eyes.

"Yes, ma'am. I have rooms starting at $2 a night, with private bath," he stated brightly.

I nodded, pulling out a wad of cash, but not letting it show too much. "And what would $5 a night get me?"

His pupils doubled in size at the question. It was obvious he hadn't expected me to ask such a question.

Fool.

"A king size bed, radio, desk, private bathroom with tub, and a spectacular view of the city," he responded.

"I'll take it."

I handed him the money, and he set the key onto my palm. "Up the elevator to the fifth floor. Make a right and room 505 is a few doors down."

I smiled back at him. "Thank you."

Carrying my dress bags, I got into the elevator and found my room with ease. I'd tip the clerk well for his assistance. When I opened the door to my new home for the next three days, I was astounded. The word "spectacular" did not do this view any justice. It was somehow as striking as the canyon, but on a different level.

This will do nicely. Low profile, yet central to the nightlife we'll need to blend into. And that view is fucking amazing!

I hummed an agreement, lacing my fingers across my stomach as I stared up at the cracked ceiling. With a place secured, I could relax and start putting some plans into motion for my hunting activities over the next few nights.

My stomach issued a low grumble, reminding me that I hadn't properly eaten since Millie's Home Cookin' hours ago. There was the lounge in the lobby. Maybe they served food as well. If not, I was sure there were restaurants in the immediate area. This evening would provide the perfect opportunity to begin acclimating to the city and the nightlife.

A wicked grin crept across my face as I imagined myself out amongst the crowds, blending in as just another pretty face while keeping my eyes peeled for suitable targets. After the mostly isolating drive across the country, the prospect of being amidst so much life was intoxicating.

My thoughts turned specifically to the type of man I'd envisioned before. The one with dark hair, a boyishly goofy sort of grin, warm and funny. Yet also the kind who would eagerly invite me back to his room for what he assumed would be a night of pleasure, only to get much more than he bargained for.

I could picture his cute face, but still not so clearly. I could see his eyes twinkling with lascivious intent as he bought me drinks and lavished compliments and innuendo my way. The briefest flicker of trepidation shot through me as I wondered if I'd feel any guilt whatsoever over torturing and killing someone like that. Likely not—after all, he would just be another foolish man daring to underestimate me, Amelia fucking Earhart. He would get exactly what was coming to him.

Still, a small part of me hoped he might prove more challenging than the weak and drunken Noonan had been back in Yuma. I would need to stay sharp while refining my skills as a torturer. That slight thrill of risk unleashed an adrenaline rush already simmering in my veins.

My hand drifted unconsciously to the small bag containing my lone tool— the kitchen knife I'd procured from Freddy's kitchen. I'd pick up a set of pliers and maybe some rope tomorrow. I shivered as my fingers brushed across the unyielding steel, savoring the anticipation of what was to come.

A fierce hunger unlike anything I'd ever tasted before welled up within me as the reality of my plans solidified. More than just a casual exploration of my darkness, this would be a re-birthing into my full, true form as death's emissary, with a hapless man as a mere tool for me to carve into.

I vowed that by the time I left this city behind, my skills would be sharpened to a razor's edge— he perfect warm-up before moving on to George, whose betrayals had awoken me to this path in the first place. I licked my lips, giving myself over fully to the bloodlust and the hot flush of excitement coursing through my body.

Yes, this was exactly what I needed. Chicago would blindly bear witness to my ascension before the world itself bowed before a reborn Amelia Earhart, dark goddess of oblivion unchained at last.

Fourteen

I TOOK LONG PULL from my glass of red wine, letting the rich liquid roll around my tongue as I surveyed the semi-crowded jazz lounge once more. The low-slung room seemed to undulate with the slow, smoky rhythms pouring from the stage. Drunken laughter and animated conversations created a steady buzz over the smoky haze.

My eyes continued roving across the writhing bodies, unconsciously appraising each man I encountered through the warped lens of my unique needs. Too old. Too slight of build. Too slovenly. Nothing about the men struck the right chord to demand further consideration.

With a disappointed sigh, I swirled the remaining wine in my glass before downing the remnants in a single gulp. The dry, fruity aftertaste seemed to linger on my tongue as I dabbed at the corners of my mouth with a linen napkin. I knew this outing was likely going to be fruitless before it even began—I knew I had time to waste—but a small flicker of hope had burned that tonight might be the night I found someone special.

These places are prime hunting grounds, my dear. You know we have plenty of time. The perfect specimen will reveal himself eventually. You haven't even scratched the surface of the city's underbelly yet tonight. Besides, didn't you decide on staying almost a week?

I exhaled slowly, tamping down my growing annoyance as my gut instincts warned me tonight would be a wash. "I did, and perhaps you're right," I muttered under my breath. "Though I confess, I don't understand what makes these idiots so difficult to identify at a simple glance."

A snort of derision sounded within my mind. *Because you're selling them far too short, my naive friend. These walking phalli have mastered superficial blasé exteriors despite their lecherous true selves simmering just underneath. The real trick is motivating each specimen to shed that mask.*

I cocked an eyebrow, unconsciously smoothing a hand over my dress as I considered her words. "You mean to purposely provoke them into revealing their true, piggish natures." I fought back a laugh. "How did I not see that?"

Precisely. Dainty little acts of vulnerability and weakness that trigger those protective—or predatory—urges. Quite like lambs wriggling free of their pens at the slaughterhouse. The same acts you gave George...

A wicked smile slowly creased my lips as the full weight of that deliciously perverse wisdom washed over me. Why should I waste time attempting to discern their individual depravities through mere silent appraisal? The key would be to manipulate each potential target into voluntarily exposing their inner darkness for me to feast upon.

Regardless, I still had that one type on man in my mind. He would be the one.

Reinvigorated, I rose from my barstool and allowed my hips to sway in an exaggerated, sultry strut as I worked my way through the undulating crowd. My fingers toyed with the folds of my soft dress, slowly exposing a hint of creamy thigh with each tantalizing step. Sharp eyes followed me, some merely admiring while others suddenly looked up like predators scenting prey.

I drifted through the throngs of people, making occasional eye contact and offering coy smiles to those whose fleeting interest had begun percolating into undisguised lust. A few of the bolder wolves whistled their appreciation or tossed out crude endearments as I sashayed by. But still, none of them managed to rise above the general din of mediocrity in my estimations.

"Slimy bastards," I whispered.

Perhaps sensing my continued lack of enthusiasm, my inner darkness suggested a new tactic. *Amelia, dear, why don't you affect some more sensuality?*

"How would I do that? My dress covers much of me, and I didn't bring red lipstick with me." I smiled, faking over my frustration.

Instead, I opted to play the damsel in distress game. With a subtle nod, I allowed my path to wobble slightly as if intoxicated, nearly colliding with a hefty young man in a faded denim jacket. His arm instinctively shot out to catch me before I careened into him fully.

"Woah there, darlin'!" He exclaimed in a thick Midwestern twang. "You alright? Maybe you should saddle up and call it a night before ya hurt yourself."

I clasped his forearm lightly, gazing up at him with feigned glassy adoration. "Oh sir, you are too kind. I fear I may have overindulged a touch on the giggle waters this evening."

He threw back his head with a loud guffaw at my overwrought parlance. "No foolin', honey! That sure would explain the lack of land legs goin' on with you tonight."

I suppressed an eyeroll at his condescending tone and oafish manner, instead aiming for a timid, eyelash-fluttering display of innocent gratitude. "Well, thank you for catching me, sir. I must be getting back now," I said as kindly as I could muster. He definitely was not the one.

The denim bumpkin shot me what he clearly assumed was a suave, winning smile. "Tell you what, baby, just lemme waltz you out to a nice quiet corner, and I'll summon you a car-riage back to your chambers post haste."

Ugh, get away from him. Do whatever you need to. He is fucking vile and, while he does deserve to be taught a lesson, maybe dropping more than one body in this city within a few days is a bad idea.

"You think?" I muttered sarcastically under my breath.

Shaking my head and pulling away gently, I replied. "I thank you for the offer, and again for breaking my fall, but I really must be going." The word "really" dripped with contempt.

He stared at me, fully understanding what I'd just said, but refusing to let me go so easily.

"No need to fret over payment, little lady. Just doin' the gentlemanly thing and all..."

Okay, Amelia. Let him have it, if you must. This is pathetic and disrespectful.

"Sir," I began, "I've told you twice now that I must be going. This will be the third, and I warn you, I will begin to yell if you do not release my arm right this minute..."

Revulsion and bile rose in my throat as he leaned down to sloppily capture my mouth, his thick tongue probing like a battering ram seeking entry. I deftly turned my head at the last second to avoid the kiss, nearly gagging on the overwhelming cloud of rancid stench rolling off his body.

My hands rose to his shoulders and I pushed him away with all my might. He stumbled backward, right onto a dancing couple. The woman screamed in pain, while the man with her tugged the fat man I'd just pushed. A screaming match between the two men began. Instead of leaving right away, I stood there, amused.

I sincerely hope that pig fucker gets what's coming to him.

"Me too, friend. Me too."

I hung around for a few more moments—until the blood started flying from fists to faces. The fat man was being destroyed by the little guy. I loved a good story of underestimation. Not so different from my own, I supposed.

I pursed my lips in annoyance as I slipped out of the lounge and back into the hotel lobby.

"Is everything all right?" The clerk asked as I rushed past the desk to the elevator.

I nodded. "Yes, thank you. I'm all right. However—" I turned to look at the lounge "— you may want to dial the police. There's a fight in there."

He picked up the phone without another word, nodding his thanks to me. I nodded back, and spun toward the elevator once more.

"That was close," I stated once the doors had closed.

It was. But you handled it well. Pity he wasn't what you were looking for. He certainly deserved every bit of torture you want to dole out...

"Yes, but again, too many bodies in a short time does not bode well for us."

The elevator dinged and the door opened just as I closed my mouth. Waiting to exit was the one I'd imagined for days now.

Fifteen

He was taller than me, though not by much. His dark hair was neatly styled with a bit of pomade holding a few rogue strands in place. He wore a crisp white dress shirt and a navy blue suit jacket that hugged his thin shoulders just right. As our eyes met, he flashed me a warm, boyish grin that sent my heart aflutter.

This really was him. The one I'd envisioned and awaited. All this time, I didn't think my imagination could manifest into reality, yet here he was.

I knew in that instant that my long search—the one that had only just begun—was over. He was my reward for persevering through the monotonous country drive up to this point. The fates had conspired to place this perfect specimen right in my path with impeccable timing.

My tongue traced my lips hungrily as I drank in his every detail. His strong jaw was lightly stubbled, just enough for a pleasantly coarse texture. Those expressive hazel eyes sparkled with a roguish charm that hinted at a fun-loving spirit lurking underneath. The man oozed an easy confidence without being off-putting. Utterly disarming and unassuming, yet ripe with untapped darkness waiting to be plucked and savored.

As the elevator doors slid open, he extended a hand while cocking his head in an inviting gesture. "After you, miss."

The polite timbre in his voice sent tingles cascading down my spine. It was rich and smooth, evoking images of brandy being poured over the rocks. And with three simple words, he'd prompted my imagination to bloom with all manner of lascivious inner visions. I swayed my hips as I stepped into the elevator, ensuring his male gaze couldn't help but track the sashay of my curves.

"Why thank you, kind sir."

He flashed another knee-weakening grin as he began to exit. Our bodies grazed against one another's with electrifying friction. My senses grew heightened by his closeness, the rich notes of his cologne tickling my nostrils while his mere presence sent shockwaves ricocheting through my core.

Reaching out to hold the door open, he leaned in and whispered, "I hope you don't mind me saying so, miss, but you look absolutely radiant this evening."

My breath hitched in my throat at his words and close proximity, my carefully crafted poise momentarily abandoned. He struck me as every bit as suave in person as I'd envisioned. And now that he was here in the flesh before me, the aura of mystery about what wicked surprises he might be harboring underneath only grew more intoxicating.

Pull yourself together, dear. Don't lose your edge and blow this now.

I cleared my throat and turned to face him fully, instinctively widening my stance in a subtle power play as if showcasing my ownership of this small space. Meeting his gaze evenly, I allowed a mischievous smirk to crease my lips.

"And you, good sir, possess quite the serpent's tongue with your honeyed words," I purred in a low, throaty voice.

He chuckled warmly, not in the least bit taken aback. "A charming lady such as yourself deserves to be plied with praise. Though I confess, you also deserve far more elaborate compliments than my limited repertoire can properly provide."

I arched an eyebrow playfully. "In that case, you'll simply have to make it up to me with deeds instead of words."

As the words exited my mouth, the weight of their innuendo and implication washed over me. My own boldness surprised me for a split second before my will strengthened in tandem with the darkness beckoning within. This was really happening, and going far better than I could have hoped.

My nameless suitor's eyes gleamed as my provocative response clearly landed home. Those sharp hazel orbs shone with a sudden predatory glint, his demeanor shifting subtly as he leaned in closer still. Our faces were mere inches apart now, his warm breath feathering across my lips as he spoke in a low, conspiratorial tone.

"Well then, in that case, might I suggest we celebrate this auspicious encounter over drinks?" He looked at his feet, then back at me. "Say tomorrow night? 7 pm? We can meet in the lounge here." He looked over toward the lounge, and my gaze followed. The police had arrived. I smiled slyly, wiping it from my face when the man turned back to me.

My heart thudded powerfully in my chest as I nodded slowly. This was it. He was taking the bait of his own free will, unaware of the all-consuming nightmare into which he was wading. A wicked smile split my features as my hand slid up to rest coyly upon his jacket lapel.

"That sounds lovely," I purred. "I didn't catch your name."

"Forgive me," he said, sticking his hand out, "I'm Anthony Fredrickson."

I gave him my hand in return. "Amy Edwards."

He kissed my hand, bid me goodnight, and the elevator doors closed

Well done, Amelia. You've most definitely found your perfect prey. Just don't get too carried away playing beforehand. We have bigger plans for this one beyond simple pleasure.

The elevator dinged open, jarring me from my heated reverie.

"I'm aware," I said. "After all, I'm the one who dreamed him up."

With that, I inserted the key into my door and walked inside. Here I could converse with my darkness better, and without anyone overhearing.

"You seem to think I've forgotten why we're here. You're mistaken," I huffed, unzipping my dress.

I was in complete control here. Not her.

Apologies, Amelia. I only wanted to help.

"Help? Help how? By annoying me? You've succeeded."

I washed my face and changed into my sleeping gown, then sat at the desk to journal.

Father,

I feel so pretentious, though it is for good reason...
I wish you could see the city of Chicago with me. It's beautiful and loud and busy.

I miss you.

Amelia

I missed him terribly, though I was glad he wasn't around to see what I'd blossomed into. That I'd fully become who I was meant to be. A tear rolled down my cheek, and I wiped it away. My annoyance and frustration with my darkness now gone.

I closed the book and climbed into bed. My darkness wisely chose to remain silent as I stared at the ceiling. The last thing I heard before falling asleep was the sounds of car horns honking.

Sixteen

MY DREAMS WERE PLAGUED by visions of Anthony—his disarming smile, those penetrating hazel eyes that seemed to bore into my soul, the rich timbre of his voice caressing my ears with its silky tendrils.

I tossed and turned, sheets tangling around my legs as imaginary scenarios played out in my mind's eye. Anthony pinning me against the elevator wall, his lips hot and insistent upon my neck. His hands roaming, groping, our breath commingling in ragged gasps and moans of delirious pleasure.

I awoke with a start, heart pounding and a thin sheen of sweat coating my skin. Sunlight filtered through the gauzy curtains, the muted thrum of the city's morning rhythms reaching my ears. Groggily, I fumbled my way out of the twisted sheets.

With a frustrated groan, I flopped back against the pillows and let my mind drift. Another restless night's sleep, my slumber held hostage by lurid fantasies of finally claiming my long-sought prize after so many weeks of meticulous planning. After tediously maintaining my veneer of polite mundanity, lest my true nature bleed through and jeopardize everything.

It had all led to this—a chance to indulge in my deepest, darkest compulsions without restraint. To claim a level of power and domination few could ever fathom, much less experience firsthand.

Suddenly feeling far too awake and energized to remain in bed any longer, I swung my legs over the side of the mattress and padded into the bathroom. As the hot water pelted my face, I couldn't resist picturing Anthony's strong jaw slick with moisture, rivulets trailing down the taut column of his neck and sculpted collarbones. Shuddering at the thought, my eyes drifted downward to take in the graceful male form fully manifested in my mind's eye.

Steam billowed around me in a humid cloud as my hand traced languorous paths across my dampened skin, savoring the frissons of sensation each teasing caress invoked. Past experiences served as mere pale imitations—impotent facsimiles in the face of what awaited me now. The notion lent a feverish intensity to my motions, stoking the slow burn of anticipation simmering within.

At last sated, I exited the steamy confines of the shower and toweled off briskly before dressing for the day. As I perused my modest wardrobe options, I found my mind wandering back to that charged elevator encounter. Relishing the recollection of Anthony's ardent gaze raking over my curves with undisguised hunger. Practically feeling the heat of his breath ghosting across my lips as our bodies brushed together amidst the promise of his blatant overtures.

A tantalizing smirk tugged at the corners of my mouth as I pictured how the evening would unfold. Anthony was utterly clueless—completely unaware of the inescapable web into which he'd stumbled and the role I had meticulously crafted for him. After weeks spent fantasizing and refining every minute detail, his presence would finally allow me to transcend to a higher echelon of decadence and indulgence. To fully inhabit the depths of my most unrestrained psyche.

My reverie was interrupted by a brusque rapping at the door. Furrowing my brow in slight confusion, I crossed the room to peer through the peephole.

Housekeeping.

Of course. They had no way of knowing I'd awoken only a half-hour earlier.

"Apologies, but I'm not quite decent! Please return a bit later if you wouldn't mind," I called out in as polite a tone as could be mustered. Footsteps retreated into the hallway as I turned back toward the room.

Over the next few hours, I made a dedicated effort to occupy myself with typical touristy activities—wandering about the hotel's opulent lobby spaces and browsing through an assortment of high-end boutiques clustered within. Yet no matter how engaged my mind may have appeared in such mundane pursuits, the irresistible allure of the shadows beckoned incessantly.

Determined to properly experience Chicago, I spent the late morning and early afternoon exploring some of the city's iconic attractions. I wandered along the riverwalk, taking in the sleek lines of the steel and glass high-rises contrasted against the historic limestone buildings. The Architecture River Tour proved enlightening, with the guide regaling our group with fascinating facts about the pioneering designs and innovative construction methods employed over the past two centuries.

From there, I ventured into Millennium Park, meandering through the sprawling green spaces and marveling at the famous Cloud Gate sculpture—a seamless, mirror-polished elliptical form that distorted and reflected the surrounding skyline in whimsical, fluid contortions. The nearby Crown Fountain's video sculptures provided a clever bit of interactivity and whimsy amidst the park's grandeur.

After enjoying a classic Chicago-style hot dog smothered in all the "required" toppings, I devoted the afternoon hours to wandering the Art Institute's hallowed halls. From the surprisingly modern and thought-provoking works to the classical masterpieces that drew millions to bask in their presence, the museum's galleries never failed to inspire and provoke introspection with each new piece encountered.

However, it was Anthony's presence in my mind that sharpened the senses and stoked the ravenous hunger lurking within. The mere notion of having secured such perfect prey, of finally having the opportunity to act upon my darkest machinations after interminably biding my time, lent an electric undercurrent to everything.

My musings persisted in their heated fantasy as the day slipped away in anticipation of evening's arrival. Of at last being able to relish the depths of such long-seeded compulsions. To revel in the intoxicating power such indulgences promised. To spend time with Anthony, though I would not kill him tonight.

Seventeen

THE DAYLIGHT HOURS CRAWLED on at an agonizing pace as I alternated between feigning interest in Chicago's assorted tourist draws and surrendering to the deliciously wicked fantasies swirling through my mind. Just imagining the surprise that awaited Anthony that evening—or possibly the next—was enough to set my pulse racing with delectable anticipation.

At long last, twilight began spilling its rich amber glow across the city skyline visible through the floor-to-ceiling windows lining the hotel's lobby. I settled into one of the plush sofas with a glass of cabernet, casually scanning the handful of patrons milling about as I awaited Anthony's arrival.

Precisely at 7 o'clock, I spotted him stride through the ornate double doors, hands stuffed into the pockets of his tailored slacks as he cast an almost nonchalant gaze about the space. Our eyes met and I felt an involuntary shiver of excited menace course through me as that now-familiar half-grin quirked his lips.

"Good evening, Miss Edwards," he purred in that impossibly smooth tone I'd been relishing the memory of all day. "You look positively radiant tonight. Though I must confess, my excitement at our reunion is disrupting my composure somewhat."

The suggestive lilt in his voice conjured all manner of scintillating scenarios as I drank in his perfectly prepared appearance—the crisp blue button-down shirt, the tailored navy suit that sculpted his lean frame so impeccably, the hint of sandalwood cologne that wafted through the air with each subtle movement.

"Why, thank you kindly, Mr. Fredrickson," I replied in my sexiest voice, making a show of allowing my gaze to leisurely roam the length of his body before returning to his eyes. "I'm rather pleased my humble efforts have managed to render you discombobulated."

He let out a chuckle as he settled onto the adjacent sofa, angling his body toward mine in a decidedly unsubtle manner.

"You give yourself far too little credit, my dear. A true natural beauty requires no elaborate embellishments—and you exemplify that ideal exquisitely." Anthony leaned in almost as if we were conspiring, the sudden proximity causing his cologne to envelop me in olfactory intoxication. "Though I must confess, the promise of your delightful company this evening is what made sleep utterly elusive for me last night."

A flicker of movement in my peripheral vision drew my attention toward the ornate wooden bar along the far wall. The immaculately dressed bartender wordlessly set about preparing our typical beverages, no doubt having received instructions from the hotel staff regarding Anthony's preferred drink.

I matched Anthony's beckoning posture, pursing my lips in an devilish half-smile. "Why, Mr. Fredrickson, I do declare I experienced similarly...restive nocturnal wanderings in anticipation of our rendezvous."

As if on cue, the bartender materialized beside our sofa setting a tumbler of amber liquid garnished with a cherry before Anthony before turning to me with a crisp, efficient nod. I accepted the proffered glass of deep burgundy wine with a murmur of thanks, never once breaking my heated, locked gaze with my evening's company.

Anthony's sculptured lips creased into a wolfish grin as he raised his glass in a toast. "To auspicious new connections, and wherever this wondrous evening may lead us."

Our beverages met with a dulcet clink, the sound seeming to reverberate through the tense, charged air between us as potently as a starter's pistol.

You two are making me sick.

Tonight's overture was officially underway, rife with deliciously sinister promise. The first cracks appeared in our smooth surfaces, inviting the essence of my true, uninhibited self to come through with thrilling delight.

Anthony drained half his tumbler in one studious draw, his gaze never wavering from mine over the rim of the glass. As he lowered it back to the coffee table with a dull clink, he let out an exaggerated sigh of satisfaction. "Delicious. Though I must admit, the drink itself pales in comparison to the company I'm savoring this evening."

My cheeks flushed with coy delight at his words, feigning girlish embarrassment despite the molten lust kindling within me. "You'll make me blush with such intense flattery, good sir." I allowed my eyelashes to dip coyly as I sneaked a sip of the rich cabernet. "Though I have no doubt your euphoric regard for me is born of a mere surface-level appreciation for my physical form."

Anthony tsked softly, head shaking in melodramatic reproach as he echoed my feigned demureness. "Now, now,

Miss Edwards—I won't hear a word slandering your seemingly endless array of admirable qualities. While your outer beauty most assuredly ensnares the senses, it's that quicksilver mind and bewitching spirit that has thoroughly enthralled and beguiled me."

The husky sincerity of his tone sent an involuntary shudder cascading through me. I could have drowned in the mesmerizing pull of those hazel depths as our gazes remained locked, heavy with the exquisite tension thickening the air between us. Part of me hungered to simply pounce—to unleash my pent-up feral side and indulge in the wanton delights that had danced through my fevered imaginings for so long.

But, no. Allowing the anticipation to fully compound and ripen would only elevate the ultimate sweetness of my victory, once claimed.

Clearing my throat with a delicate rasp, I matched Anthony's sensual timbre with one of velvet. "Well, aren't you simply overflowing with tantalizingly honeyed words this evening?" I allowed my eyelids to drift shut momentarily as I let the words drizzle from my lips. "One might be lulled into believing a sweet-talking charmer such as yourself has laminated his tongue with the varnish of a hundred honey bees."

When my eyes reopened, Anthony's had darkened perceptibly—his dilated pupils all but eclipsing the hazel irises in a swirling maelstrom of desire. A muscle danced along the chiseled line of his jaw as his gaze tracked the path of my tongue slowly tracing my lower lip.

"You make a valid point, my dear," he murmured in a voice gone husky with want. "One which, I fear, could only be definitively proven through further extensive research into the matter." A sly grin split his beautiful mouth as he leaned closer.

The sudden heat of Anthony's thigh pressing against mine sent a delicious frisson of electricity arcing through me. I held his stare brazenly as my tongue idly toyed the plump pucker of my lips.

"Well, as an intrepid scholar yourself, Mr. Fredrickson, you must feel professionally obliged to apply due diligence in satiating your curiosities." I punctuated the graveled statement by allowing my hand to rest upon his knee—kneading the firm musculature there with maddeningly languid motions.

Anthony's breath escaped in a harsh exhalation as his eyelids fluttered, the fingers of one hand flexing spasmodically against the plush sofa cushion. When his gaze collided with mine once more, I was enraptured by the wanton avarice etched across his chiseled features.

In one sinuous motion, he reached up to brace his hand against the nape of my neck—his thumb caressing the pulse point below my ear in rhythmic counterpoint to the steady throb now pounding between my legs. Anthony's lips hovered a breath from mine as his words fanned searing tendrils across my inflamed skin.

"Well then, we'd best not stall in conducting our...research, had we?" His tongue swiped across his lower lip in an unconscious mimicry of my mannerism moments before. "Lest our combined intellectual curiosity fester into overwhelming distraction."

My own desire-thickened response stuck in my throat as Anthony abruptly closed the minimal distance separating us—his mouth slanting over mine in a devastating kiss that obliterated any residual power of coherent speech.

This was no simple, tentative meeting of lips. No tiny exploratory brush of restrained lust. This was a full-scale assault of pure, unadulterated want and possession. Anthony's free hand cradled the back of my skull as our mouths warred in delirious, open-mouthed fervor—his tongue lashing with insistent undulations that robbed me of any pretense of composure.

I matched his ferality with unleashed abandon, raking my nails gently across the nape of his neck as I arched languidly into his embrace. Every stoked synapse screamed with desperation and primal need unbound. Anthony's robust frame radiated a searing virility as our bodies molded together with escalating urgency.

I didn't see this coming, but it is a wonderful precursor to seeing him again tomorrow...then killing him.

At last, he tore his mouth from mine with a guttural groan—our mingled exhalations commingling in scorching pants amidst the heavy silence now blanketing us. Those hazel depths bored into me, the avarice I glimpsed there sending dizzying thrills of lust spiraling through my core.

"I don't know about you, but I'm gripped by an overwhelming compulsion to relocate our "research" to more private accommodations." The words dripped from Anthony's lips in a rough growl that flooded my senses with fresh arousal.

Part of me wanted nothing more than to forsake all propriety and simply straddle his lap here in the hotel lounge. To do things with a man I hadn't in far too long. The primal rut I'd fantasized about for so torturously long now hovered within exhilarating reach.

No, the path toward utter domination and Anthony's complete enthrallment required more calculated measures. Harnessing the lustful urges would amplify the sweet obliteration to come.

Feathering my fingertips along the thrumming pulse-point at his throat, I matched Anthony's ardent stare through a gilded fan of lashes. "I believe that would be a most prudent course of action, Mr. Fredrickson. Perhaps we could adjourn to my private quarters and strategize further upon our scholarly initiative?"

With a growl torn from the deepest recesses of desire, Anthony latched onto my wrist and yanked me bodily atop his waiting lap. There would be no further ambiguity or pretense.

The final veneer of civility had shattered—replaced by untamed greed and unrestrained need.

Eighteen

Anthony's growl reverberated through me as his arms enveloped my waist, pulling me fully onto his lap. Our bodies melded together in a heated embrace, his arousal evident against my inner thigh. I could feel the pounding of his heart through the thin fabric of his shirt as my fingers raked up his chest.

"To your room?" I murmured against the stubbled line of his jaw, allowing my lips to graze his skin.

His response was to stand abruptly, cupping me against his chiseled frame as he strode with purpose toward the elevators. I clung to his shoulders, savoring the raw masculinity radiating from him. A few other hotel patrons turned startled glances our way, but Anthony paid them no mind.

The elevator doors had no sooner slid closed before his mouth crashed into mine again, all restrained pretense incinerated in the inferno of our passion. My back met the wall with a gentle thud as his hands roamed freely, stoking the aching need coiling inside me.

We tumbled out into the hallway in a flurry of tangled limbs and hungry caresses. I led the way to my suite, our trail marked by discarded clothing. Anthony's jacket and shirt puddled near the door, my dress following soon after.

I pulled him atop me onto the luxurious bed, our kiss deepening as he pinned me deliciously beneath his weight. His sculpted muscles rippled against my bare skin as our bodies moved in an age-old rhythm. For this moment, the world contracted to just the two of us entangled in sinful ecstasy.

Afterwards, we lay spent yet sated, harsh breaths gradually slowing. Anthony's arm was draped possessively across my waist as I traced aimless patterns across the taut slopes of his chest. A profound sense of peace enveloped me, despite the turmoil I knew still lay ahead.

Anthony's deep voice rumbled against my back. "That was...utterly sublime."

I tilted my head to meet his molten hazel gaze. "Indeed it was. Though I must confess, I'm almost embarrassed at how ardently I've craved this intimacy." My fingers toyed idly with the short hair at his nape. "You've bewitched me utterly, Mr. Fredrickson."

His full lips quirked into a lopsided smile as he brushed a few stray tendrils from my flushed cheek. "And you've held me in thrall since the moment we met, my dear Miss Edwards. Though I suspect there are depths to you yet unplumbed..."

His voice trailed off meaningfully. I felt my heart stir with an unnameable emotion - part affection, part dread for what lay ahead. Turning in his arms, I traced the sharp line of his jaw, allowing the pad of my thumb to graze his lower lip.

"Perhaps it's best those depths remain submerged, for now," I murmured, leaning in to capture his mouth in another lingering kiss. "Some mysteries are meant to be savored gradually."

Anthony's rumbling chuckle vibrated against my lips. "A sagely point, my love. Very well, I shall revel in unveiling you one delicious layer at a time."

We lapsed into contented silence, limbs intertwined amid the tousled sheets that still bore the musky tang of our lovemaking. My mind briefed on the mission ahead - the plan that had been set into motion.

But for this suspended moment, I allowed myself to bask in the serene aftermath, pushing thoughts of the future aside. Because deep down, I could no longer deny that a part of me had become increasingly, inexplicably enraptured.

The gentle rise and fall of Anthony's chest lulled me into a tranquil haze. His fingers trailed lazily along the curve of my spine, raising gooseflesh in their wake. I nuzzled deeper into the warm hollow of his neck, inhaling the faint traces of his cologne mingled with the musky remnants of our passion.

In this cocoon of intimacy, it was easy to momentarily disregard the larger machinations in play. To simply exist in the moment and bask in the afterglow of the profound connection we'd shared. A part of me longed to freeze this singular fragment of time forever - to somehow insulate us from the harsh realities lurking just on the periphery.

Eventually, my languid musings were disrupted by the low rumble of Anthony's voice cutting through the stillness.

"You know, this entire evening has felt almost...dreamlike." He shifted beneath me, drawing back just enough for our gazes to meet. "As though I've somehow transcended into a parallel plane where all societal constraints and preconceptions have fallen away."

I cocked an inquisitive eyebrow. "Oh? And how does that make you feel?" My fingers idly toyed with the dusting of hair along his chiseled chest. "Liberated? Unshackled from the trappings of the 'real' world?"

"Precisely." He caught my wandering hand, bringing it to his lips to dust a series of feather-light kisses along the knuckles. "Though I must admit, it's not merely the freedom from inhibition that bewitches me so. It's the intimation that in this space, I've been granted a glimpse into the unvarnished depths of your soul."

I felt my breath hitch at the unexpected profundity of his statement. Those hazel eyes bore into me with an intensity that threatened to unmask the carefully cultivated facade I'd been maintaining - the intricately constructed veneer of coquettish mystique.

"You give me far too much credit, Mr. Fredrickson," I countered with a teasing lilt, desperate to deflect away from the disquieting impact his words had triggered. "I am but a simplistic creature motivated by the most rudimentary of impulses and whims."

"No..." He shook his head adamantly, refusing my attempt at evasiveness. "I refuse to accept such spurious self-deprecation. There is a richness and complexity burning within you, my dear—an intoxicating paradox of seeming fragility sheathing an unshakable core of fortitude."

His fingers had drifted to cup the line of my jaw, fingertips grazing my lips with tantalizing reverence. "You are a singularly captivating enigma, Amy Edwards. And I'll admit, the prospect of unraveling the layers comprising your essence has firmly enthralled me."

The molten sincerity blazing in Anthony's stare detonated a kaleidoscope of conflicting emotions within me. Uncertainty, bemusement, but predominantly a keen sense of discomposure at having been seen—truly seen—by this perceptive man with whom I'd inexplicably become entangled, emotionally and physically.

I opened my mouth to respond, though what I'd intended to say I'll never know. For at that moment, a strident buzzing reverberated from the bedside table, shattering the suspended tension surrounding us. I felt Anthony tense subtly beneath me as we both instinctively turned toward the source of the intrusion.

With a soft curse, I disentangled myself from his embrace and padded across the plush carpet, all too aware of my nude form in the ambient glow filtering through the gauzy curtains. I picked up the receiver and told the caller to wait a moment. No one knew who I was, let alone that I was here, save the front desk clerk.

I spun back toward the bed where Anthony had propped himself into a sitting position, sheets bunched rakishly around his waist.

"I should probably take this," I murmured, averting my gaze from the searing intensity still flickering across his chiseled features.

Anthony inclined his head, seeming to understand the abrupt shift in my demeanor. "Of course. I'll make myself comfortable here while you attend to whatever you need to."

Tonight's blissful suspension was over.

I sat on the chair at the desk, answering the questions the clerk had for me regarding last night's altercation inside the lounge. He informed me he would relay my responses to the police in an effort to help me keep anonymity.

After the call ended, I went into the bathroom and snapped back to reality, chiding myself for allowing this. He was but a toy, as plaything in my quest to fully transform into my true, dark self.

Ah, there you are, Amelia. I was beginning to wonder if I'd lost you.

"You have not. I have not. Tomorrow, Anthony shall meet his fate."

Nineteen

I STEPPED BACK INTO the bedroom, my bare feet gliding across the plush carpet. Anthony had shifted to lounging against the tufted headboard, sheets draped rakishly across his lap in a way that simultaneously concealed and tantalized. His tousled chestnut locks and the satisfied curve of his lips broadcast the lingering afterglow of our passionate tryst.

"Everything alright?" He murmured, hazel eyes heavy-lidded yet trained intently upon me.

I allowed my gaze to roam his chiseled features as I approached the bed, buying a moment to realign my mind-set after the jarring phone call. "Yes, just...handling a minor logistical matter."

With an inscrutable smile, I crawled onto the mattress and repositioned myself atop the cover beside him. Anthony's arm snaked around my waist as I nestled into the Haven of his sculpted frame, my back cradled against the firm musculature of his chest.

"Good, I'm glad there are no pressing concerns to distract us from this sublime interlude." His gravelly timbre caressed the sensitive whorls of my ear, each rumbled syllable seeming to reverberate through my very core.

I turned my head to gaze up at him through the gauzy fan of my lashes. "You seem quite entranced by our intimacy this evening, Mr. Fredrickson."

His full lips quirked in a lopsided grin. "Understatement has never been one of my weaknesses, has it?" One calloused fingertip traced the delicate plane of my collarbone with meandering reverence. "Though in this instance, I'm afraid euphemistic trivialities would be a disservice to the utterly wondrous exchange we've experienced."

My cheeks flushed with a potent mixture of titillation and venerating pride. Even in the throes of carnality, Anthony possessed an unparalleled gift for spinning desire into rich, silver-tongue poetry. An ability to elevate base lust into the lofty echelons of philosophic ideals - sensual existentialism painted in broad, sumptuous brushstrokes.

"You have a uniquely verbose yet intoxicating way with words, my dear," I husked, arching my back in a languorous stretch that allowed my backside to press more fully against the insistent arousal cradled at his groin. "One could become thoroughly bewitched by the tides of your verbal sorcery."

Anthony's chest expanded with an audible inhalation, his free hand drifting down to splay across the flat plain of my abdomen. "If my words possess any true enchantment, it is merely a dim flicker compared to the blazing, primordial pull of your presence." His palm kneaded idly at the toned musculature beneath as he dipped his face into the ebony cascade of my hair. "You ignite an insatiable desire within me, Amy—awaken a ravenous greed to plunder the uncharted depths of your smoldering mysteries."

His unabashed candor set off fireworks of exhilaration through my neural pathways. I twisted sinuously in his arms until our fronts were fused together, my fingers tracing the chiseled V of his hipbones that vanished beneath the rumpled bedding.

"Is that so?" I purred in a voice rendered husky with escalating need. "Well then, I believe further diligent examination is in order."

Anthony's plump mouth descended upon mine in a searing kiss of blistering possession and feral abandon. The slick glide of his tongue lashing insistently against my own obliterated any residual coherence as our limbs intertwined with mounting urgency. My nails raked down the muscled expanse of his back, inciting a guttural groan from deep within his chest.

When finally we parted, twin shudders of breath fluttering across swollen lips, Anthony's enlarged pupils had all but eclipsed the hazel of his irises. His features flushed with hormones and desire, the tendons of his throat straining with tension.

"You, my love, are utterly bewitching," he growled in a cadence gone gruff and visceral. "Dangerously, lethally, devastating in your unrepentant allure."

I held his brooding stare, feeling the ever-roiling tempest of my own emotions swell within my breast. Desire, tangled inextricably with something more inscrutable. Something that hinted at a looming precipice I was rapidly approaching—an inescapable conclusion I'd been subconsciously steering toward since the evening Anthony Fredrickson had first insinuated himself into my world.

Tilting my chin upward in a subtle challenge, I brushed the pad of my thumb across the kiss-reddened swell of his lower lip. "You consistently underestimate yourself, dear Anthony. Have you never considered that perhaps you are equally culpable for the enchantments lashing us in this wanton snare?"

His brows arched in an expression of cynical amusement. "I am but a pawn, enraptured and lured mindlessly by the grand spectacle you orchestrate." One soft finger traced the contour of my cheek, skimming down the line of my throat to settle against my thundering pulse. "You are the true sorceress here, my love. I am simply hapless quarry to the vast reaches of your charms."

I forced a slight, ironic smile to hide the unease his statement had caused me. . With deliberate focus, I shifted my position so that I was straddling Anthony's lap, bedsheets twisting around my bare waist like murky silk waves. His hands settled reflexively at the flare of my hips with a possessive insistence that set my core pulsing with renewed fervor.

"Perhaps we've snared each other, then," I murmured, leaning closer to trace the stubbly line of his jaw with the tip of my nose. I allowed the words to dissolve between us as my lips hovered a breath from his. "Wound irretrievably in an intractable web spanning far beyond notions of hunter and prey."

Anthony inhaled sharply, his pupils engulfing me in a maelstrom of blazing lust and adoration. "No bounds, no limits," he growled. "We shall unravel each other down to the dusky, untapped wellsprings of our truest selves."

Twin shock waves reverberated through me—one celestial, one mercilessly grim. For that declaration rang both like the sweetest of promised intimacies, as well as a foreboding pronouncement of something much more ominous descending. My grip tightened at his shoulders, nails digging into flesh as our mouths clashed together once more.

All thoughts fragmented into splinters of searing heat and implosive ecstasy as our bodies rejoined with unbridled fervor. In that enraptured haze, I found myself straddling the precarious edge of an abyss.

So close, so terrifyingly near the inescapable point of no return.

Twenty

Dawn crept through the curtains. I stirred, Anthony's arm heavy across my waist. Last night's memories flooded back. Drinks. Dancing. Heated glances that promised more.

I slipped from bed, careful not to wake him. The bathroom mirror revealed smudged makeup and tangled hair. Cold water shocked my system awake. I stared at my reflection, searching for answers, realizing we'd stayed in bed all of yesterday.

Back in the bedroom, I dressed quietly. Anthony slept on, peaceful and unaware. I watched him, conflict churning in my gut. He'd become more than a mark. More than I'd bargained for.

Remember why you're here, Amelia.

I did. But things had changed. I'd changed.

Anthony stirred. "Amy?" His voice was thick with sleep.

I forced a smile. "Good morning."

He reached for me. I let him pull me close, breathing in his scent. For a moment, I allowed myself to forget everything else.

"Thought you'd left," he murmured.

"I'm here," I said. It wasn't entirely a lie.

We lay in silence, his heartbeat steady against my cheek. The sun climbed higher, painting the room in warm light.

You're getting too close. Cut him loose, pun intended.

Maybe. Maybe not.

Anthony's stomach growled, breaking the spell. We laughed, tension dissolving.

"Breakfast?" He suggested.

I nodded.

We left the hotel, morning air crisp and invigorating. Anthony took my hand. It almost felt natural. Dangerous.

The diner buzzed with activity. Over coffee and eggs, we talked. About everything. About nothing. I found my-self opening up, yet also holding back. He'd never know who I really was.

Anthony listened. Really listened. His eyes never left mine.

For the first time in years, I felt seen. Understood. Accepted. For things I was not.

This isn't the plan, Amelia...

After breakfast, we walked through a park. Children's laughter filled the air. Anthony's arm around my waist felt like home. And a trap I was half-willingly walking into.

"I have to leave town tomorrow," he said suddenly.

My heart skipped. "I'll be leaving in a few days, anyway. At least we met and got to know each other."

He squeezed my hand. "I'll miss you."

"I'll miss you too," I forced out of my mouth.

We stopped by a fountain. Anthony turned to face me, expression serious.

"Come with me instead," he said.

I blinked. "What?"

"Come with me. What do you have to do that's so important?"

My mind raced. This wasn't supposed to happen. None of it was.

Amelia... Say no. Finish what you started.

"Anthony, I can't. I have people expecting me," I lied.

His face fell, saddened that I couldn't simply drop everything for him.

We spent the walk back to the hotel in silence. Anthony was brooding, while I was playing out the scenario of things I'd be doing to him tonight. He wouldn't be going to New York.

As evening fell, we found ourselves back in my hotel room. Anthony ordered room service while I showered, washing away the day's sweat and grime. Under the hot water, my thoughts swirled.

Amelia—

"I know," I said. "Have you not caught on to the fact that I'm going to get him to take us back to his place tonight under the pretense of 'I'd like to see it' and kill him there?"

I could almost hear her smile in my head.

Good. I quite like this plan.

I dressed in a simple black dress, applied minimal makeup. When I emerged from the bathroom, Anthony's eyes lit up.

"You look beautiful," he said softly.

We ate on the balcony, the city spread out below us like a glittering carpet. The conversation flowed easily, punctuated by comfortable silences.

As we finished dessert, Anthony reached across the table and took my hand.

"I know this is crazy," he said. "We've only known each other a short time. But I feel like I've been waiting for you my whole life."

My heart raced. Part of me wanted to punch him.

But I needed to play the part.

I squeezed his hand. "I feel the same way."

We ate in silence before I piped up again.

"You know, we've spent all of our time together in my room. It would be nice to see your place before you go."

He looked at me quizzically, then smiled.

"You're right. Let's go after we finish dessert."

Once we were finished, we left the room service cart outside of my room, and joined hands as we walked to the elevator.

Have you thought about how impractical that dress is? Jesus, Amelia.

The night was as gorgeous as the twinkling lights around the city center. We held hands, laughed, and talked on our short walk to Anthony's apartment.

We stopped in front of a beautiful Brownstone. Anthony let got of my hand and motioned toward the front door.

"This is it," he said, grinning, and taking a step up.

"It's lovely," I said, starting to walk up the stairs with him.

I suppose we'll have to duct tape his mouth shut so the neighbors don't hear...

A predatory smirk briefly crossed my face as Anthony unlocked the door and guided me inside.

We entered a dimly lit foyer with mailboxes in the wall on the left side.

I didn't bother to pay attention to the names and apartment numbers, as I'd be killing a resident, and that was all that truly mattered.

"Upstairs," Anthony said as he placed a foot on the first stair.

I nodded and followed, listening for neighbors. I didn't hear anything.

Could we be so lucky?

I didn't know, but I hoped we were.

Anthony stuck his key in the lock of one of the two doors, twisted the key, then opened the door. I could hear everything, even a pin drop. There really were either no people home unless they were sleeping. No matter. He was a man, so he had to have something I could keep his mouth closed with. It was well-known men did not have the same threshold for physical pain women did. That was why we gave birth, not them.

I wasn't sure where I was going to find the supplies I needed in Anthony's apartment. Who would keep rope in their bathroom?

You can open closets.

Now I had to figure out how to open the closets without him seeing or hearing. Did my darkness think I was Harry fucking Houdini? I quietly chuckled at the absurdity.

Once inside, Anthony turned around to lock the door behind me.

"How about a tour?"

"I'd love one." I smiled.

This was the start of a night we'd never forget.

Twenty-One

The apartment was nothing to write home about; it was a typical male dwelling. The couch was brown leather, there was a radio against the far wall, and a coffee table. The walls were barren, devoid of life.

He led me into the kitchen, just off the living room. Another bare room with white walls, cabinets, and a refrigerator. The stove looked untouched, as though he'd never used it. No surprise there, he was a salesman who traveled most of the time.

"And now to the best room in the place," he said, walking down a short hallway that had a single closet and another doorway for the bathroom.

He opened the bedroom door, and much to my nonplussed reaction, it was a sight of complete desolation. Bare white walls, a bed and dresser, with a closet built into the wall at the foot of the bed. He did have a side table with lamp, but he truly lived the minimum. And why not? He was rarely home to enjoy much else. I considered myself fortunate to have met him.

I was on the edge of incapable of complimenting the place, when he interrupted my thoughts.

"I know," he started, "It's not much, and, in my defense, doesn't need to be. I'm so often on the road for work—"

"—I understand. How often are you in town, anyway? I feel so fortunate to have met you at all," I cut in with a forced smile. I was growing impatient. I needed to find pliers and rope. A rag was easy enough to find.

He pondered my question a moment, then responded. "If I'm lucky, seven days a month."

That sounded absurd to me. Even in my height of fame, I'd been home more than that. I couldn't say that out loud, however.

"Wow, you must really love your job to sacrifice so much," I purred, warming him up.

"I do," he replied, turning the light out and closing the bedroom door behind us as we walked toward the living room.

This is perfect.

"Oh! Would you mind if I used your bathroom to freshen up?" I asked.

"Go right ahead. Ill make us a cocktail and see you in the living room."

I nodded and ducked into the bathroom. A rag was easier to find than I'd imagined—it was sitting right on top of the sink.

I opened the linen closet, unsure of what I'd find, but the universe had been smiling on me. I saw a small toolbox and carefully opened it. Sitting on top of a hammer was a pair of needle-nose pliers.

Now we're in business. But how will we secure the rag in his mouth?

That was a good question, so I dug around the toolbox and found some rope. It wasn't very long, maybe twenty or so inches, but it would have to suffice. I placed the implements into my purse, checked myself in the mirror, and exited the bathroom.

Anthony was waiting for me on the couch, as promised. I eyes the kitchen on my way to the couch, hoping I'd missed a chair or stool. No such luck. I smiled painfully at him.

"Always a gentleman," I said, taking the offered glass from his waiting hand.

We clinked and sipped, then I set mine down on the coffee table, twisting to face him as I sat back up.

"Close your eyes, I've got a surprise for you."

Anthony eyed me warily then chuckled.

"I'm serious," I said.

He huffed. "Okay." Then closed his eyes.

I straddled him, placing my knees on his fingers.

"Ouch! Amy, that hurts."

"Don't worry, darling, I'm almost done. You're going to love this."

I backhanded him across the face then shoved the rag into his mouth and quickly wrapped and tied the rope around.

Anthony tried to speak, the only sounds being moaning. His eyes shot open, fear engulfing them. He tried to push me off of him, but when he did, just by his own force and twisting, broke both of his hands. Now he was moaning louder.

I threw my head back and laughed. "Moron," I chided. "You thought I was just some bimbo you could lure with sweet words and sleep with. Lucky for you, that's now why you're going to die."

Amelia, quit talking and get to work already. He needs to know nothing.

"I know that, but it's more fun this way, no?"

Anthony cocked his head to the side, wondering if I was speaking to him. I ignored the movement and got to work, pulling the pliers from my purse and grabbing one of his hands.

He made a whole lot of noise that sounded like he was trying to plead with me not to do whatever I was about to do. I looked him in the eyes and grinned. Words would have been a waste, so I got down to business.

It was much more difficult than I'd imagined it would be. I struggled to even break one of his fingernails with the pliers. And boy did Anthony scream, or try to, the whole time. I kept at it anyway, hoping I'd be able to accomplish something. I didn't have the want or time to soak his hands in warm water first—this was already messy enough. Fingernails bleed a *lot*.

Amelia, come on. Just kill the man already. This is boring.

"You're right. It *is* boring. Let me just find..." I trailed off as I lifted the bottom of my dress to pull the knife from the waistband of my undergarments.

Anthony wailed again. I backhanded him across the face again.

"Shut up! You men are all such babies. Can't handle the sight of a knife. The last man I killed with this cried, too."

Again I grinned, this time with malice. I traced the tip of the knife down his cheek, following a teardrop, then down his chest, stopping right around his heart. I teased and played with the tip, casually slicing bits of skin here and there. The more he whimpered and whined, the more pleasure I got.

AMELIA! Just fucking kill him already!

I huffed out a "fine," raised my arms, gripping the knife with both hands, and brought them down as hard as I could. I heard a crack and the knife sunk in.

"Was that a rib? Interesting."

Anthony's eyes had gone momentarily wide before his head dropped back lifeless.

I watched as the last bits of life left him, then cleaned myself and the knife in the kitchen. I placed the knife in Anthony's cutlery drawer, smiling. They'd never know it wasn't even his.

Twenty-Two

I LEFT THE BROWNSTONE with a heavy heart, the weight of my actions pressing down on me as I walked back to my car. The night air was cool, a stark contrast to the heat of the emotions swirling within me. The city lights blurred as I fought back tears, knowing that Anthony was no longer alive.

Upon reaching my hailed taxi, I took a deep breath and sat behind the driver, telling him where when he asked. I rode through the noisy streets of Chicago, my mind replaying the events of the night. When we reached my hotel, I quickly got out and headed to my room, locking the door behind me as if trying to keep the ghosts of my past at bay.

I leaned against the door, closing my eyes and taking a moment to collect myself. The room was dimly lit, casting long shadows that seemed to mock my solitude. I walked over to the bed and sat down, the events of the past few days crashing down on me.

Anthony had been different. He wasn't just another target; he had become someone I cared about, despite my initial intentions. My actions had been meticulous, but my feelings had complicated everything. Now, I was left with a mix of guilt and relief, knowing that what I had started was finished, but at what cost?

I changed into bedclothes and washed my face, trying to erase the evidence of the night. As I looked at myself in the mirror, I barely recognized the woman staring back. My reflection seemed hollow, my eyes devoid of the spark that had once driven me.

Still beautiful, Amelia.

I sat on the edge of the bed, running my hands through my hair. I needed to move on, but I couldn't bring myself to think about it just yet. Instead, I lay down, staring at the ceiling, my darkness refusing to quiet.

Amelia, we did precisely what we came here to do. You imagined this man as your next victim, and lo and behold, he was real. This was his purpose.

"You're right. That doesn't mean I didn't develop feelings for him."

I closed my eyes and drifted off to sleep.

The next morning, I woke up feeling no more rested than I had the night before. I dressed quickly, my movements mechanical. The hotel room felt suffocating, and I knew I needed to leave. I packed my things, trying to keep my mind focused on the task at hand.

As I checked out, the clerk gave me a polite smile, unaware of the turmoil beneath my calm exterior. I stepped out into the bright morning light, squinting against the sun. The city was waking up around me, oblivious to the darkness I carried.

I made my way to a small café down the street, hoping a cup of coffee might help clear my mind. The café was quiet, the morning rush not yet in full swing.

I took a seat by the window, watching the world go by as I sipped my drink.

My thoughts drifted back to Anthony. I remembered our conversations, the way he had looked at me with genuine interest. It had been a long time since someone had seen me, not *truly* seen me but still, beyond the façade I presented to the world. For a brief moment, I had allowed myself to believe in something more, but reality had a way of crushing such illusions.

I knew I couldn't dwell on the past. I had a life to continue, and I needed to stay focused. But as I sat there, staring out at the bustling street, I couldn't shake the feeling that something had fundamentally changed within me. I had always been able to separate myself from my victims, to see them as mere marks. But Anthony had broken through those barriers, and now I was left grappling with the aftermath.

With a sigh, I finished my coffee and stood up. I had to move forward, even if I wasn't sure where I was headed. I paid for my drink and stepped back into the street, the city's noise enveloping me. I had a long drive ahead and a new place to prepare for. But as I walked away, I couldn't help but glance back one last time, a small part of me wondering what might have been.

I drove out of Chicago, the city fading into the distance as I headed east. The drive to Rye, New York, was long and uneventful, giving me too much time to think. I tried to distract myself with the radio, but my mind kept wandering back to Anthony. I replayed our final moments together, the look in his eyes when he realized what was happening. I had seen fear in my victims before, but this time it was different. This time, it hurt.

When I finally reached Rye, I felt a mixture of relief and dread. The small town was a stark contrast to the bustling city I had left behind. I found a nondescript motel near the edge of town and checked in. The clerk was a middle-aged woman with graying hair and a kind smile. She greeted me with a warmth that felt foreign and unwelcome.

"Good evening, dear. How long will you be staying with us?" She asked.

"Just a few nights," I replied, forcing a smile as I took the key. "Thank you."

The room was small but clean, a temporary sanctuary from the storm inside me. I set my bag down and sat on the bed, staring at the walls. I knew I should plan my next steps, but instead, I allowed myself to sink into the mattress, my mind drifting back to Anthony's face, his final moments etched into my memory.

With a heavy sigh, I stood up and began to unpack. Tomorrow, I would start learning George's new ways, follow the plan, and continue my life. But tonight, I allowed myself a moment of reflection, a brief respite from the relentless march of my existence.

As I lay down to sleep, I knew that the coming days would not be easy. But for the first time in a long while, I felt a glimmer of something unfamiliar: doubt. I wondered if there was another way to live, a path that didn't involve death and deception. The faces of my victims haunted me, each one a reminder of the life I had chosen.

The next morning, I woke up feeling a sense of determination. I dressed quickly and left the motel, deciding to take a walk through the town. It was small and quaint, with tree-lined streets and friendly faces. I felt out of place, a wolf among sheep, but I was also curious. There was something about the simplicity of the town that called to me.

As I wandered, I found myself in a small park. I sat on a bench, watching children play and couples stroll by. The normalcy of it all was jarring, yet oddly comforting. I felt a pang of longing, a desire for something I had never allowed myself to consider: a normal life.

No one recognized me, providing a sense of relief. I spent many years here, so for not one person to realize Amelia Earhart was alive was a blessing.

I spent the day exploring the town, letting myself be a part of it, if only for a little while. By evening, I felt a strange sense of peace, though the weight of my past was never far from my mind.

Back in my motel room, I sat on the edge of the bed, the journal unopened beside me. I knew I should write in it, prepare myself for the next move. But instead, I stared at the wall, lost in thought. Anthony's face was the one I saw most clearly, his final moments a haunting reminder of what I had done.

With a heavy heart, I picked up the journal and walked to the desk. The details were familiar, the routine almost comforting in its predictability. But as I wrote more, a part of my mind remained distant, questioning, wondering if there was another way.

I finished writing and set the journal aside. Tomorrow, I would start my preparations, follow the plan, and continue my life. But tonight, I allowed myself a moment of reflection, a brief respite from the relentless march of my existence.

As I lay down to sleep, I knew that the coming days would be challenging, coming to a final climax and then...

For the first time in a long while, I felt a glimmer of hope, a small spark that maybe, just maybe, I could find a way out of the darkness.

Twenty-Three

I WOKE UP THE next morning feeling a mixture of determination and dread. I dressed quickly, pulling on a pair of jeans and a simple shirt, and left the motel room without bothering to make the bed. The small room had served its purpose, but I couldn't bear to stay there any longer. I needed to get out, to breathe fresh air, and to clear my mind.

The town of Rye, New York, was just beginning to wake up as I stepped out onto the street. The sun was still low in the sky, casting long shadows across the pavement. I started walking, my steps purposeful yet unhurried, as I took in my surroundings. The town was quaint, with tree-lined streets and charming old buildings that spoke of a long history. I felt a pang of longing, a fleeting desire for a simpler life that I knew I could never have.

I wandered through the quiet streets, passing by small shops and cafes that were just opening for the day. The air was crisp and cool, carrying the scent of fresh bread and coffee. I found myself drawn back to the small park in the center of town. It was a peaceful oasis, with neatly trimmed lawns, flower beds, and benches scattered about. I sat down on one of the benches, watching as the town slowly came to life around me.

Children started to appear, running and laughing as they made their way to school. Parents walked by, chatting with each other or on their phones, their minds occupied with the day's tasks. I felt like an outsider, a spectator to a world that was not my own. But for a moment, I allowed myself to imagine what it would be like to be part of this world, to have a normal life.

My thoughts drifted back to Anthony. I remembered our conversations, the way he had looked at me with genuine interest. It had been a long time since someone had seen me—truly seen me—beyond the mask I presented to the world. For a brief moment, I had allowed myself to believe in something more, but reality had a way of crushing such illusions.

I knew I couldn't dwell on the past. I had a life to continue, and I needed to stay focused. But as I sat there, staring out at the bustling street, I couldn't shake the feeling that something had fundamentally changed within me. I had always been able to separate myself from my victims, to see them as mere marks. But Anthony had broken through those barriers, and now I was left grappling with the aftermath.

With a sigh, I stood up and started walking again. I needed to keep moving, to keep my mind occupied. I wandered through the town, letting myself get lost in its winding streets and hidden corners. The architecture was charming, with old colonial houses and quaint storefronts that seemed frozen in time.

Eventually, I found myself standing in front of a small café. The sign above the door read "Emma's Café," and the smell of freshly brewed coffee wafted out as someone opened the door. My stomach growled, reminding me that I hadn't eaten since the night before. I decided to go in, hoping a cup of coffee and something to eat might help clear my mind.

The café was cozy and inviting, with wooden tables and chairs, and a display case filled with pastries and cakes. I ordered a coffee and a croissant, then found a seat by the window. As I sipped my coffee, I watched the world go by outside. The town was fully awake now, people bustling about their daily routines.

I couldn't help but feel a twinge of envy as I watched them. They all seemed so content, so at ease in their lives. I wondered if they knew how lucky they were, or if they took it all for granted. I had chosen my path long ago, but that didn't stop me from wondering what might have been if I had made different choices.

As I finished my breakfast, I knew I couldn't stay in the café forever. I had to keep moving, to stay ahead of the darkness that always seemed to be nipping at my heels. I paid for my meal and stepped back out into the street, feeling a bit more grounded but still restless.

I spent the rest of the day exploring Rye, letting myself be a part of it again, if only for a little while. I visited the local library, wandered through a few antique shops, and even took a stroll along the beach. The ocean was calm, the rhythmic sound of the waves soothing my frayed nerves.

By evening, I felt a strange sense of peace, though the weight of my past was never far from my mind. Back in my motel room, I sat on the edge of the bed, the journal unopened beside me. I knew I should write in it, prepare myself for the next move. But instead, I stared at the wall, lost in thought. Anthony's face was the one I saw most clearly, his final moments a haunting reminder of what I had done.

With a heavy heart, I picked up the journal and walked to the desk. The details were familiar, the routine almost comforting in its predictability. But as I wrote, a part of my mind remained distant, questioning, wondering if there was another way.

I finished writing and set the journal aside. Tomorrow, I would start my preparations, follow the plan, and continue my life.

After putting the journal away, I decided to take another walk, this time through the quieter residential areas of Rye. The homes were charming, each with well-kept lawns and flower beds that added splashes of color to the street. I could hear the faint sounds of children playing in backyards, the hum of a lawnmower, and the occasional bark of a dog. It was a stark contrast to the noisy, chaotic life I had left behind.

As I walked, I thought about my next steps. I needed to blend in, to become a part of this community if only for a few days. I had learned over the years how to adapt quickly, to become whoever I needed to be. But this time, it felt different. There was a part of me that wanted to stay, to come home and rebuild something here.

Lost in thought, I almost didn't notice the elderly woman who waved at me from her front porch. She had a kind face, framed by white hair, and she smiled warmly as I approached.

"Good evening, dear," she called out. "Lovely night for a walk, isn't it?"

I nodded and returned her smile. "It is. This is such a beautiful town."

"It is indeed," she said, her eyes crinkling at the corners. "I'm Eleanor. I've lived here my whole life."

I introduced myself, giving her the name I had chosen for this place. "Nice to meet you, Eleanor. I'm Amy."

"Welcome to Rye, Amy," she said. "If you ever need anything, don't hesitate to ask. We're a friendly bunch around here."

"Thank you, Eleanor," I replied. "I appreciate that."

As I walked away, I felt a strange sense of comfort. Eleanor's kindness was a stark reminder that there was good in the world, even if I had been living in its shadows for so long.

I returned to the motel, feeling a bit lighter. Tomorrow would be another day, another chance to start anew. For now, I would take things one step at a time, allowing myself to believe that maybe, just maybe, there was a way out of the darkness that had consumed my life for so long.

Twenty-Four

THE NEXT MORNING, I woke up with a clear sense of purpose. George Palmer Putnam had wronged me, and now it was time to make things right. After a quick shower, I dressed in comfortable clothes that allowed me to blend into the crowd. I grabbed my gear—binoculars, a notebook, and my camera—then headed out.

The sun was just beginning to rise as I made my way to Emma's Café. I needed a strong cup of coffee to kickstart the day. The café was already bustling with early risers. I ordered my coffee and a scone, then found a table near the window where I could watch the world go by.

As I sipped my coffee, I thought about GPP and his wife, Jean-Marie Cosigny James. They were well-known figures in Rye, NY, with their fingers in many pies. But behind their public personas, there were secrets—secrets I intended to uncover.

I spent the morning familiarizing my-self with their schedule. George and Jean-Marie were creatures of habit, which made my task easier. George typically left for his office around 8:30 a.m., while Jean-Marie had a more var-ied schedule, involving charity work and social events.

After finishing my coffee, I headed to their neighborhood. Their house was in an upscale part of Rye, surrounded by similarly grand homes. This was not the house I lived in with him. This one was more elegant somehow. I parked a few blocks away and found a bench in a small park nearby that offered a clear view of their front entrance.

At precisely 8:30 a.m., George emerged from the house, dressed in a sharp suit and carrying a briefcase. He got into a black car, driven by a chauffeur, and they drove off. I noted the time and direction they headed, then turned my attention back to the house.

Jean-Marie appeared shortly afterward, accompanied by a woman who looked like a personal assistant. They got into a silver sedan and drove off. I decided to follow them, keeping a safe distance to avoid detection.

They drove to a local community center where Jean-Marie had a meeting scheduled. I waited in my car, watching as they entered the building. These meetings usually lasted a couple of hours, so I used the time to scout the area, noting potential escape routes and vantage points.

When Jean-Marie and her assistant finally emerged, they headed to a nearby café for lunch. I took a seat at an outdoor table across the street, positioning myself so I could observe them without being seen. They talked animatedly, their conversation filled with laughter and ease. It was clear Jean-Marie was well-liked and respected in her community, which made my task more challenging.

After lunch, they returned to the Putnam residence. I spent the rest of the day observing the comings and goings at the house, noting any patterns or unusual activity. By late afternoon, George returned home. He and Jean-Marie greeted each other warmly, a picture-perfect couple.

Gross.

"You're telling me!"

But I knew better. I knew the man behind the mask. George had a dark side, and I was determined to expose it.

The next few days followed a similar pattern. I tracked their movements, gradually building a comprehensive picture of their daily lives. George spent most of his time at his publishing company, meeting with authors and attending business lunches. Jean-Marie was busy with her charitable activities and social events.

Despite their predictable routines, I remained cautious. I kept my distance, parking in places they wouldn't see me, and if they did, I was one of many silver Packard 120s. It was a delicate balance, maintaining my cover while gathering the information I needed.

One evening, as I was discussing the plan with my darkness, I noticed something odd. George and Jean-Marie had scheduled a private dinner at an upscale restaurant in town, but there was no mention of any specific occasion. It seemed out of the ordinary for a couple who usually spent their evenings at home.

We'll need to follow them, see what they're up to. Good thing we hadn't planned that night to kill them, huh?

I sneered in spite of myself.

"Well, yeah, I suppose you're right. But I'm certainly itching to."

As am I, Amelia. As am I.

I arrived at the restaurant early, choosing a discreet table near the back where I could observe without being noticed. The restaurant was elegant, with dim lighting and an intimate atmosphere. It was the kind of place where people went to celebrate special occasions or discuss important matters.

Haven't we been here before? We did live here...

"Come to think of it, yes, we have. Good thing no one recognized us."

GPP and Jean-Marie arrived promptly at seven. They were seated at a table near the center of the room, clearly enjoying each other's company. As they talked and laughed, I tried to read their lips, hoping to catch snippets of their conversation.

After a while, George's expression grew serious. He leaned in closer to Jean-Marie, speaking in hushed tones. Her smile faded, replaced by a look of concern. I wished I could hear what they were saying, but the ambient noise of the restaurant made it impossible.

Their dinner continued for over an hour, and by the end, Jean-Marie seemed more relaxed. I was sure the bottle of wine helped. They paid the bill and left, walking arm in arm. I followed them out, keeping a safe distance as they returned to their car.

Instead of heading home, they drove to a secluded spot by the beach. I parked a short distance away and watched as they got out and walked along the shoreline. The moonlight reflected off the water, casting a soft glow on the scene. They stopped at a bench overlooking the ocean, sitting close together and talking quietly.

It was a beautiful, intimate moment, and for a brief second, I felt a pang of guilt. I was intruding on their private lives, turning their genuine connection into just another mark. But I quickly pushed the feeling aside. This was personal. George had to pay for what he'd done to me, to Amelia.

As I watched them, I noticed something peculiar. George took something out of his pocket and showed it to Jean-Marie. She nodded, her expression serious again. They continued talking, and I could see the tension in their body language. Whatever they were discussing, it was important.

I stayed until they finally got up and returned to their car. It was late, and I needed to get back to the motel to review what little information I had gathered. As I drove away, my mind raced with possibilities. What could be so important that they had to discuss it away from prying eyes?

Back in my room, I conversed with myself and my darkness. There was nothing concrete to go on, just a sense that something significant was happening.

Amelia, what does it matter? We're going to kill them one way or another.

"I know, but now I can't help but wonder if someone will interrupt us."

Then we need to kill them soon. Very soon.

"I agree."

The next day, I returned to my surveillance, but this time, I focused more on their interactions and the people they met. George had a meeting at his office with a group of men who looked like business associates. They stayed for a few hours, and when they left, I managed to snap a mental pictures of them. I might need to identify these men later.

Jean-Marie's day was filled with her usual activities, but she seemed distracted, her mind elsewhere. I followed her to yet another charity event, where she mingled with guests and gave a speech. She was charming and eloquent, but I could see the underlying tension in her eyes.

Fucking goody-two shoes she is.

I laughed.

That evening, I decided to try something bold. I had obtained a lock-picking device, and made my way into their house. I hid in the bedroom closet.

It was past ten when GPP and Jean-Marie returned home. They were talking heatedly as they came up to the room, and I listened intently, hoping to catch something useful. At first, all I could hear was muffled voices, but then George's voice became clearer.

"...can't keep doing this, Jean-Marie. It's too risky."

"I know, but we don't have a choice," she replied, her voice strained.

"There has to be another way. We need to be careful. If anyone finds out..."

The conversation trailed off, and I cursed under my breath. They were hiding something, but I didn't have enough information to piece it together. I would need to be patient, to continue observing and waiting for the right moment.

The following days were uneventful, with George and Jean-Marie sticking to their usual routines. I kept a close eye on them, hoping for another clue, but nothing significant happened. It was frustrating, but I knew I couldn't rush things.

Amelia, I'm telling you this does not matter. Let's just kill them now.

I knew she was right, so I stayed quiet until I was mostly sure they'd fallen asleep. I snuck out of the closet, down the stairs, and out the front door. I made sure to turn the lock on the doorknob so George wouldn't know anyone had been in the house.

Back in my room, staring at the ceiling from bed, I made a final decision.

"They die tomorrow."

Twenty-Five

THE NEXT MORNING, I woke before dawn, my mind clear and focused on the task ahead. There would be no more surveillance, no more waiting. Today was the day George Palmer Putnam and Jean-Marie would face justice for their sins.

I dressed in dark, nondescript clothing and packed a small bag with the essentials: gloves, a flashlight, the tools I'd need to gain entry, and the knife. As I prepared, my darkness hummed with anticipation.

Finally, Amelia. We've waited so long for this.

"I know," I whispered, double-checking my supplies. "But we need to be careful. One mistake could ruin everything."

I left the motel while the sky was still dark, driving to a spot near the Putnams' house where I'd hidden a second car days earlier. I'd use this vehicle for my escape, leaving no connection to the motel or my aliases.

As I waited for the neighborhood to stir, I ran through the plan one last time. George would leave for work around 8:30, as usual. Jean-Marie had a charity luncheon scheduled for noon. The house would be empty by then, giving me time to slip inside and prepare.

The sun rose, painting the sky in hues of orange and pink. I watched as lights flickered on in nearby houses, people beginning their morning routines. At 8:30 sharp, George emerged from the house, briefcase in hand. He climbed into his waiting car and drove away, oblivious to the fate that awaited him.

Jean-Marie left an hour later, looking elegant in a pale blue dress. As her car disappeared around the corner, I allowed myself a small smile. Everything was proceeding as planned.

I waited another thirty minutes to ensure the coast was clear, then moved my car closer to the house, parking it in a secluded spot that offered a clear view of the back entrance. From here, I could keep watch and make my move when the time was right.

The day stretched on, each minute feeling like an eternity. I occupied myself by going over the plan again and again, visualizing every detail. My darkness kept me company, whispering encouragement and stoking the flames of my resolve.

Remember why we're here, Amelia. Remember what he did to us.

I closed my eyes, memories flooding back. The betrayal, the pain, the life that had been stolen from me. My hands clenched into fists, nails biting into my palms. "I remember," I whispered. "And he'll pay for all of it."

As the afternoon wore on, I watched the neighborhood through binoculars. Children returned from school, dog walkers strolled by, and delivery trucks made their rounds. I noted each passerby, assessing potential witnesses or obstacles.

The sun began its descent, casting long shadows across the manicured lawns. At 5:30, right on schedule, Jean-Marie's car pulled into the driveway. She emerged, arms full of shopping bags, and disappeared into the house.

An hour later, George's car arrived. From my vantage point, I could see him through the windows, moving from room to room. The couple's silhouettes appeared in the kitchen, going about their evening routine.

As darkness fell, lights flickered on in the house. The glow from the windows spilled onto the lawn, creating pools of warm yellow against the encroaching night. I watched as George and Jean-Marie settled in the living room, their figures occasionally passing before the curtains.

My heart raced as I glanced at my watch. It was almost time. I took a deep breath, steeling myself for what was to come. This was the moment I'd been waiting for, planning for, dreaming of for so long.

It's time, Amelia. No more hesitation. No more doubt.

I nodded, my resolve hardening. "You're right. It ends tonight."

Silently, I exited the car and retrieved my bag from the trunk. The tools inside clinked softly as I slung it over my shoulder. I paused, scanning the quiet street one last time. All was still, the houses around me dark and silent.

I crept across the lawn, keeping to the shadows. The grass was damp beneath my feet, and the night air carried the scent of blooming flowers. It seemed almost peaceful, a stark contrast to the violence I had planned.

As I approached the house, I could hear the muffled sound of the television through an open window. George and Jean-Marie's voices drifted out, punctuated by occasional laughter. They sounded happy, content. Oblivious.

I pressed myself against the wall beside the back door, my hand reaching for the lock-picking tools in my bag. This was it. The point of no return. Once I crossed this threshold, there would be no going back.

My fingers closed around the cold metal of the lock pick. I took a deep breath, steadying my nerves. The darkness within me surged, urging me forward.

Do it, Amelia. Open the door. Claim your vengeance.

I raised the tool to the lock, poised to begin. But something made me hesitate. A fleeting memory, perhaps, or a last-minute doubt. I froze, my hand trembling slightly.

In that moment of hesitation, a sound broke the silence of the night. A twig snapped somewhere behind me. I whirled around, my heart pounding, searching the darkness for the source of the noise.

Was it just an animal? A neighbor taking out the trash? Or had someone discovered my presence?

As I stood there, pressed against the wall, the lock pick still in my hand, I realized that everything hinged on what I did next. The choice I made in the next few seconds would determine not just the fate of George and Jean-Marie, but my own as well.

Twenty-Six

Sucking in a deep breath, I turned back to the door, and stuck the device's tip in the lock. It made a low click when the lock disengaged. I smiled and opened the door as silently as possible.

GPP and Jean-Marie were still laughing and talking, which told me they heard or suspected nothing. I grinned wider, caressing my bag of supplies. The only thing missing was rope, which was okay by me. After all, I didn't want to be here all night torturing them. More time here meant a greater chance of being caught. And I still had a couple of things to do in Glendale.

The anticipation...

I knew what she meant. It was electrifying. I felt all of my nerves tingling. This was the whole reason I came back to The States at all. It would be relatively quick, and I would savor every moment.

I pulled the knife from the bag and dropped the rest. While they *could* take prints, would they believe that those prints belonged to a dead woman?

I didn't bother sneaking into the living room where the two were sat on the couch. Instead, I walked normally. The look on George's face was priceless when I came around the corner.

"Who are you? How did you get in here?"

I grinned, showing my teeth.

"Who am I? Oh really, George," I sat opposite them on a chair, casually waving the knife.

Jean-Marie started to move. I darted toward her, knife tip gleaming.

"Don't."

She sat back down and grabbed George's hand.

"Hang on," he started, "Do I know you?"

I stood, grinning like the Cheshire Cat.

"You do."

He cocked his head to one side, squinting. He looked me up and down. The hair was much different, but for the man I'd been married to, it shouldn't have been this difficult.

"Amelia?" He squeaked.

"And we have a winner!"

"How... What... Why..."

I waved the knife as though it was an extension of my hand.

"None of those things matter now, do they? You had me declared dead and took all of my money. Good thing I had a stash," I said. "But, since you'll be dead soon, I suppose there's no harm in answering your questions."

I walked over to the couch, grabbed the bottle of wine and drank from it, sitting down between them.

"Thanks to Freddy—he's dead, by the way, killed him myself. And Mary," I hung my head in false shame then picked it back up sharply, eyeing them in turn, absorbing their fear.

"Anyway, thanks to that alcoholic, we crashed but made it to a remote island. It wasn't the one we were headed for, but I digress. The people there were Asian, and friendly. They took us in, fed and clothed us. We lived with them for two years. Until the day I woke up to Freddy being gone. That was a few weeks ago. I stole a few planes to get back, and hunted him down. Killed Mary then Freddy."

I turned on Jean-Marie.

"Killed her because she was a witness."

Jean-Marie started whimpering.

"P-please don't."

I laughed.

"Oh would if I could. Can't have you running your French mouth now, can we?" I growled.

George sat up a bit and attempted to calm me.

"Amelia, I understand—"

"—You understand nothing!" I bellowed, turning on him, slicing his bicep open.

Both George and Jean-Marie screamed.

"You never knew who I was. You treated me like I was a meal ticket and nothing more. You paraded me in front of the newspapers and publishers, the wealthy friends and colleagues. And for what? I'll tell you what. So you could line your pockets and have more notoriety than you had before you met me. You were a simple publisher then. After? Well, you were a big shit, married to Amelia Fucking Earhart!"

I slashed again, this time across his face, bringing back down across his chest.

Jean-Marie shifted in an attempt to run. I whirled on her, slicing open her throat like a hot knife through butter. She gurgled, blood like a red waterfall down her white dress.

I paused to admire my work.

"Shame, really."

I turned back to George, who was patting the individual cuts, unsure how to get them to stop bleeding and stinging.

"Futile," I scoffed. "Besides, now that you know everything, and Jean-Marie is dead, I'll be killing *you*."

George opened his mouth to say something, and the knife flashed across his throat. He kept trying to speak, but looking more like a fish.

No sound escaped aside from more gurgles. He grabbed at his throat, accomplishing nothing more than bloody hands.

I dropped the knife on his lap, and kissed him on the cheek.

"Goodbye, old chap," I whispered into his ear.

I didn't bother to check the house for anyone or anything, I simply walked out the way I'd come in. I even closed the back door behind me after locking it. I jumped into my Packard and went back to the motel.

Once there, I packed only the things I would need; most of the new wardrobe stayed. I didn't care for or about it. Besides, what I had planned required none of that nonsense.

I loaded up my car and got back on the road for Glendale, California.

Twenty-Seven

I DIDN'T LINGER IN Rye after dealing with George and Jean-Marie. I hit the road, each mile marking the distance from my past. My Packard 120 hummed along, an abused but reliable beast. Glendale was a long way off, and I needed to be smart about my stops.

The first stretch was smooth. The hum of the engine was my only companion. But the miles took their toll. The Packard's fuel gauge dipped steadily, and I knew I had to make my first stop soon. The small towns blurred together. Each one had a fuel station with a neon sign, flickering in the twi-light.

The first stop was in a sleepy town with a single fuel station. The attendant, a wiry teenager with greasy hair and an oversized uniform, shuffled over. He was all nerves and stammering politeness. I watched as he fumbled with the pump, the fuel fumes filling the air.

"Long trip?" He asked, trying to make conversation.

"Something like that," I replied, handing over the cash. He gave me a quick smile and a nod, but his eyes never met mine. Back on the road, I let the miles slip away, the landscape barely changing from town to town.

Coffee became my lifeline. The first cup was from a dingy roadside diner, the kind of place where the coffee is burnt and the service slow. The waitress, a heavyset woman with tired eyes, poured the coffee without a word. It was strong and bitter, but it kept me awake. I gulped it down and hit the road again.

Another one hundred ten miles, another stop. This time, the fuel station was run by an older man with a face like leather and hands that had seen hard work. He didn't say much, just took my money and nodded. His silence was comforting in a way. It was a reminder that not everyone needed to know my business. I grabbed another coffee from the station's tiny counter. It was better than the last one, but not by much.

The road stretched on, a ribbon of asphalt cutting through the heartland. The Packard ate up the miles, but each one felt like a small victory. I passed through small towns with names I'd forget as soon as I saw them. Each one had its own charm, its own story, but I wasn't here for sightseeing. I was on a mission to the end.

The third stop for fuel was uneventful. A middle-aged woman with a cigarette dangling from her lips filled the tank. She had a hard edge to her, the kind that comes from living a rough life. She didn't ask questions, just did her job with practiced efficiency. I appreciated that. I grabbed yet another coffee at the diner next door—this one watery and lukewarm—and pushed on.

By the fourth stop, fatigue was creeping in. My eyes felt heavy, and my muscles ached from the hours behind the wheel. I pulled into a larger fuel station, one with a convenience store attached. I decided to stretch my legs and grabbed a coffee and a sandwich from inside. The clerk, a young woman with bright red hair, rang me up. She gave me a curious look, but didn't pry. I appreciated that.

I sat on a bench outside, eating slowly and watching the traffic go by. The sun was setting, casting long shadows across the pavement. It was peaceful, in a way. I finished my meal and got back in the car, ready to push on.

By the time I reached Toledo, I was running on fumes and adrenaline. I found a small, out-of-the-way fuel station and pulled in. The attendant was an older man with a friendly face. He didn't ask questions, just filled up the tank, and gave me a once-over like he knew I'd been through something. He handed me my change and wished me a safe trip.

Toledo wasn't just a pit stop; it was where I'd lay low for the night. The modest motel's weathered exterior featured peeling paint and a faded wooden sign. The clerk gave me a key, and I headed to my room. It was basic—bed, chair, and a bathroom that had seen better days. But it was perfect. After a quick bath, I felt human again, the hot water washing away the grime of the road.

I tossed and turned for a while, unable to sleep. The adrenaline from the past days hadn't fully worn off. I decided to take a walk, maybe find something to eat. The streets of Toledo were quiet, the kind of quiet that's both comforting and unnerving. I found a diner still open, the kind of place where the coffee is strong, and the pie is homemade. I ordered both, settling into a booth by the window.

The waitress was a chatty sort, mid-forties with a kind smile. Her name tag read "Marge." She brought over my order and asked where I was from.

"Just passing through," I replied.

She nodded, as if she'd heard that story a hundred times. "Toledo's a nice place to catch your breath," she said. "We've got the zoo, if you're into that sort of thing. And the art museum's not too shabby."

The zoo wasn't my thing, but the art museum piqued my interest. I made a mental note to check it out in the morning. For now, I just wanted to enjoy my coffee and pie in peace. Marge left me alone after that, sensing I wasn't in the mood for small talk.

Before bed, like always, I wrote in my journal. Tonight was one final letter to Edwin.

Father,

I have accomplished everything I needed to and am on my way back to you.
I love you.

Amelia

The next morning, I woke early, the sun barely peeking over the horizon. I grabbed my journal and headed out. The Toledo Museum of Art wasn't far, and it was a good way to kill time before hitting the road again. The museum was a grand building, with columns that made it look more like a Greek temple than a place full of paintings.

I wandered the galleries, losing myself in the brushstrokes and colors. Art had always been a quiet passion of mine, something George never understood. He'd mock my interest, calling it a waste of time. But standing there, in front of a painting by Monet, I felt a sense of peace. It was like the artist had captured a piece of my soul, the part that still believed in beauty and wonder.

Good riddance to the lot of them.
"Agreed."

I spent hours there, soaking in the tranquility. It was a stark contrast to the chaos that had defined my life recently. But eventually, the pull of the road was too strong. I left the museum, feeling lighter, more focused. It was time to move on, to keep heading west.

As I drove out of Toledo, I found myself reflecting on the people I'd encountered along the way. The fuel station attendants, the waitresses, the clerks—each one had played a small part in my journey. They were ordinary people, living ordinary lives. But to me, they were reminders of the world I was fighting for, the world I was trying to reclaim from the shadows of my past.

Back on the road, the miles melted away. Each stop for fuel was a reminder of how far I'd come and how far I still had to go. I made a mental map of each town, each fuel station, marking my progress. The journey was grueling, but necessary. Glendale was waiting, and with it, the final chapter of my plan.

The road stretched on, a ribbon of asphalt cutting through the heartland. The Packard ate up the miles, but each one felt like a small victory. I passed through small towns with names I'd forget as soon as I saw them. Each one had its own charm, its own story, but I wasn't here for sightseeing. I was on a mission.

Toledo had been a brief respite, a chance to catch my breath and re-group. But now, it was time to move on. The road was calling, and I had a mission to complete. George and Jean-Marie were the final act, but not the finale. That was to take place in Glendale.

I reached the next town as the sun was setting, the sky painted in shades of orange and pink. It was beautiful, in a way that made me feel hopeful. I found a small diner and ordered a meal, savoring the simple pleasure of good food.

As I ate, I thought about the people I'd met on this journey. The fuel station attendant, Marge at the diner, the museum curator. They were kind, ordinary people, living their lives. They reminded me that not everyone was out to betray and hurt. It gave me a sense of balance, of perspective.

But I couldn't dwell on that. I had a job to do, a mission to complete. I paid the bill and headed back to the motel, feeling a sense of determination. Tomorrow was another day, another step closer to my goal.

The road ahead was long, but I was ready. Each mile brought me closer to Glendale, closer to the end of my journey. I was focused, driven, and nothing would stand in my way. I was Amelia Earhart, survivor, avenger, and nothing stopped me from getting the justice I deserved.

Twenty-Eight

The highway to Glendale stretched endlessly ahead, each mile marker a reminder of how far I'd come and how much farther I had to go. Leaving Toledo, I'd felt a renewed sense of purpose. The museum's peace and tranquility had washed away some of the grime that had settled on my soul, but it was fleeting. The mission was still on my mind, and every turn of the wheel brought me closer to my final confrontation.

The first fuel stop came sooner than I'd hoped. The Packard's tank was greedy, and the miles were many. I pulled into a small, rundown gas station just outside Toledo. The attendant, a grizzled man with a tobacco-stained mustache, shuffled over. He moved with the slow, deliberate pace of someone who had seen it all and had nothing left to hurry for.

"Fill 'er up?" He asked, his voice gravelly from years of smoking.

"Yeah, and keep the change," I replied, handing him a bill. He nodded, pocketing the money with a grunt. His eyes flicked over me, but he didn't pry. It was better that way. The less people knew, the safer they were.

I grabbed a coffee from the station's dingy counter. It was thick and bitter, more sludge than liquid, but it would keep me awake. I took a gulp, grimacing at the taste, and hit the road again.

The miles rolled by in a blur of farmland and open skies. The landscape was beautiful in its simplicity, but I barely noticed. My mind was on the road, my hands steady on the wheel.

Another one hundred ten miles, another stop. This time, it was a family-run station in the middle of nowhere. The teenage boy who filled the tank was polite but curious.

"Where you headed?" He asked, wiping his hands on a rag.

"West," I said, keeping my answers short. His eyes lit up with the dreams of someone who hadn't yet been jaded by life.

"I'd love to go west someday. See the ocean, maybe get a job in a big city," he said wistfully.

"Maybe you will," I replied, giving him a small smile. It was the most I could offer. Dreams were for people who had the luxury of hope. I grabbed another coffee and drove on, the boy's dreams lingering in my mind like a ghost.

By the time I reached Des Moines, the sun was setting, casting long shadows across the city. The electric signs flickered to life, their incandescent bulbs a bright beacon of the nightlife stirring awake. I found a modest motel on the outskirts and checked in. The clerk, a young woman with bright red hair and a nose ring, handed me a key without asking questions. She was too busy with her own life to care about mine.

The room was small but clean. I took a quick bath, washing away the dust and weariness of the road. As the water flooded over me, I felt the tension in my muscles begin to ease. It was a temporary reprieve, but I'd take it. Dressed in fresh clothes, I ventured out into the city.

Des Moines had a quiet charm. It wasn't as bustling as the larger cities, but it had its own pulse, its own rhythm. I found a diner and ordered a meal, enjoying the simple pleasure of hot food and a fresh cup of coffee. The waitress, a middle-aged woman with a warm smile, chatted as she served me.

"If you're looking for something to do, Union Park is just a few blocks away," she said, refilling my coffee cup. "It's a nice place to unwind."

I nodded, making a mental note to visit. After finishing my meal, I left the diner and headed towards the park. The night air was cool and refreshing, a welcome change from the stuffy confines of the car. The park was dimly lit, the trees and other foliage casting eerie shadows on the ground. I wandered among them, letting the abstract forms distract me from my thoughts.

Each tree was unique, a testament to nature's creativity and resilience. I found myself drawn to a large, intricately knotted tree. It was beautiful and haunting, much like the life I'd left behind. I stood there for a long time, lost in thought. These were sights I'd never see again, moments of peace amidst the chaos. The end was growing closer.

The next morning, I woke early, eager to continue my journey. I packed my things, checked out of the motel, and found a nearby coffee shop. The clerk, a cheerful young man with a tattoo of a coffee cup on his arm, handed me a steaming cup of the good stuff. It was the best coffee I'd had in days, rich and aromatic.

"Long trip?" He asked, making small talk as he worked.

"Yeah, you could say that," I replied, taking a sip. The warmth spread through me, waking me up fully. I thanked him and headed back to the Packard.

The road out of Des Moines was long and dull like the trip had been thus far, the horizon a distant line that seemed to mock my progress. I stopped for fuel again, this time at a larger station with multiple pumps. The attendant, a young woman with a stern face, filled the tank quickly and efficiently.

"Anything else?" She asked, glancing at the car.

"No, that's all. Thanks," I replied, handing over the cash. She gave a curt nod and went back to her work. I grabbed another coffee from the station's convenience store, noting how the cups had different slogans printed on them. Mine read, "Adventure Awaits." How ironic.

As I drove, I thought about the people I'd met along the way. Each one had their own story, their own struggles and dreams. They were small encounters, fleeting moments that reminded me of the world I was fighting for. A world where people could live their lives without fear, without the shadows of the past haunting them.

Because you give a damn about them.

"Of course not. They just give me something to think about so I can stay awake. Besides, you haven't said much since we left Rye."

Another one hundred ten miles, another stop. This time, it was a small town with a single gas station and a diner next door. The attendant, an older man with a friendly smile, chatted as he filled the tank.

"Where ya headed, ma'am?" He asked, genuinely curious. "Cain't be here; there ain't nothin here."

"West," I said, the same vague answer as before.

"Beaut'ful countr'y out there. Safe trav'ls," he replied, handing me my change. I thanked him and went to the diner down the road for another cup of coffee. The waitress, a young woman with a tired look in her eyes, served me quickly. She had the air of someone who'd seen too much too soon, and I felt a pang of sympathy.

Back on the road, I let my mind wander. The journey was boring, but each mile brought me closer to Glendale, closer to the end of my road. I thought about George and Jean-Marie, their shocked faces still vivid in my memory. I laughed and my darkness joined in.

As I left Des Moines in my rear view mirror, I thought about the people I'd met, the brief moments of peace I'd found. My journey was coming to an end—to it's final resting place. But not soon enough.

Twenty-Nine

The Packard 120's engine purred as I left Des Moines in my rearview mirror. The landscape transformed gradually, flat prairies giving way to undulating hills, while the distant Rocky Mountains emerged on the horizon like sentinels of the West. Each mile marker was a countdown to Glendale, my ultimate destination.

My first pit stop came at a ramshackle service station on the outskirts of a for-gettable town. A gangly teenager with an unruly mop of hair shuffled out to greet me.

"Top her off?" he asked, flashing a gap-toothed grin.

"Please. And some coffee, if you've got it," I replied, handing over a few crumpled bills.

He nodded, his gaze lingering admiringly on the Packard's sleek lines. Inside, a weary-looking woman poured steaming coffee into a paper cup.

"Long haul?" she inquired, sliding the cup across the counter.

"You could say that," I answered, savoring the bitter warmth. It was a small comfort against the bone-deep fatigue that had become my constant companion.

Back on the road, the Rockies loomed larger, their snow-capped peaks glinting in the afternoon sun. Another hundred-odd miles brought me to a quaint town nestled in the foothills. This gas station was a family affair, run by an older couple who moved in perfect synchronicity.

"Where're you headed?" the husband asked as he filled the tank.

"West," I replied simply, my standard non-answer.

"Godspeed," he said, returning my change. His wife appeared with a fresh cup of coffee, her smile genuine and warm.

"Enjoy the journey," she offered. I thanked them both, their kindness a brief respite from the solitude of the road.

As dusk approached, painting the rugged landscape in hues of gold and purple, I pulled into a larger station with an attached diner. The waitress, a sharp-eyed woman with an air of efficiency, served me a sandwich and coffee without small talk.

"Passing through?" She asked, topping off my cup.

"Just another traveler," I replied between bites.

"Watch yourself in the mountains after dark," she cautioned, her tone softening. "They've got their own rules."

I nodded, grateful for her concern. The meal finished, I returned to the Packard, its headlights cutting through the gathering darkness. The moonlit silhouettes of the mountains loomed ever closer as I pressed on.

Denver materialized on the horizon, a sprawling oasis of light nestled against the Rockies' imposing backdrop. I found a modest motel on the city's outskirts and checked in. The disinterested clerk handed over a key without comment. The room was spartan but clean—a bed, a dresser, a mirror reflecting my travel-worn face.

After a quick bath to wash away the road's grime, I ventured into the city. Denver pulsed with energy, even at this late hour. The streets hummed with conversation and laughter. I ducked into a small café, relishing the luxury of a hot meal and fresh coffee. The waiter, an enthusiastic young man, insisted I visit Red Rocks Amphitheatre.

"It's breathtaking," he assured me. "You won't regret it."

I took his advice to heart, returning to the motel for a night of dreamless sleep before rising with the sun. The drive to Red Rocks was brief but spectacular, winding through terrain that seemed sculpted by divine hands. As I approached, massive red formations rose before me, framing a natural amphitheater of awe-inspiring proportions.

Parking the Packard, I made my way to the viewing area. The panorama before me was nothing short of majestic—a testament to nature's raw power and beauty. I stood transfixed, drinking in the grandeur, knowing these moments of wonder were fleeting treasures in my relentless journey.

As I explored the site, I couldn't help but imagine the legendary performances that had echoed off these ancient stones. Their legacy seemed etched into the very rock, a monument to human creativity and resilience.

Reluctantly leaving Red Rocks behind, I returned to Denver for a quick lunch at a bustling diner. The waitress, her smile as bright as the Colorado sun, set down a hearty sandwich and steaming coffee.

"Just passing through?" she inquired, her tone friendly but not prying.

"Westward bound," I replied, my standard response becoming a mantra of sorts.

Fueled by both food and purpose, I hit the road again. The Packard's engine thrummed as Denver receded in my mirrors, the landscape morphing from mountain foothills to rolling hills, then to vast, arid plains. The next fuel stop came at a lonely outpost, manned by a weathered old-timer with kind eyes.

"California, eh?" he mused as I paid, my destination slipping out for once. "That's quite a trek."

I nodded, accepting a cup of coffee that was more bitter than strong. It would keep me alert, and that was all that mattered.

The miles unfurled before me, each one a step closer to Glendale, each one taking me further from my past. Towns blurred together, fleeting snapshots of American life – a young couple running a gas station in perfect sync, a family-owned diner serving pie that tasted of home, a motel clerk whose curious glance spoke volumes.

As twilight painted the sky in deep purples and blues, I found myself on the outskirts of another nameless town. The motel was modest, but it offered sanctuary for the night. Sleep came swiftly, my dreams a kaleidoscope of faces left behind and roads yet untraveled.

Dawn broke, and with it came the familiar routine – a quick shower, a hastily grabbed coffee, and the Packard roaring to life, eager to devour more miles. The open road stretched before me, an endless ribbon of possibility and escape.

I thought back to my days as a pilot, when the sky was my domain and the earth a patchwork quilt far below. Now, the road was my runway, each town a waypoint in my journey. The mission drove me forward, unyielding and resolute.

Every fuel stop, every interaction, became a brief connection to the world I was passing through. Names and faces blurred together, but their small kindnesses lingered – a smile, a word of caution about mountain roads, a free refill of coffee for the road-weary traveler.

The Packard, my faithful companion, ate up the miles with a steady growl. We were one now, woman and machine united in purpose. The countryside unspooled around us – majestic mountains giving way to golden plains, then to desert vistas that stretched to the horizon.

Each sunset brought me closer to Glendale, to the culmination of this journey. I was Amelia Earhart, reborn on the American highway, my spirit unbroken, my determination unbowed. The road was long, but my resolve was stronger. Whatever lay ahead in Glendale, I would face it head-on, just as I had faced every challenge in my life.

As night fell and Las Vegas loomed ahead, I allowed myself a small smile. The journey was far from over, but for the first time in a long while, I felt the thrill of anticipation. Whatever tomorrow might bring, I was ready.

Thirty

CALIFORNIA-BOUND, I FELT THE pull of the West, the open road stretching out before me like a promise. Each mile brought me closer to Glendale, closer to the end of this relentless journey. The Packard 120 purred steadily, eating up the miles with a faithful hum. The landscape transformed as I crossed the Rockies and descended into the desert, the rugged mountains giving way to arid plains and endless skies.

The first fuel stop came at a dusty station on the edge of a small town. The attendant, an older man with a sun-beaten face, approached with a slow, deliberate gait.

"What'll it be?" He asked, already reaching for the pump.

"Fill, please," I replied, handing him some cash. He nodded, his eyes squinting against the bright sunlight. "Oh, and sir, where can I get some coffee around here?"

He pointed to the small store attached to the station.

Inside, the station's small café offered a respite from the heat. The coffee was strong and bitter, but it was just what I needed to stay awake. I took a long sip, savoring the warmth as it coursed through me, then got back on the road.

The desert stretched out endlessly, a vast expanse of sand and scrub brush under a blazing sun. Another one hundred ten miles, another stop. This time, it was a tiny station run by a young couple. They worked in tandem, the man pumping gas while the woman prepared coffee inside.

"Where you headed?" He asked snidely, wiping his hands on a rag.

"That's none of your business," I replied, annoyed by his tone.

"Well, I never," he said, handing me my change. His wife brought out a steaming cup of coffee, her smile genuine and warm.

"Have a good journey," she said. He gave her a dirty look. I thanked them both and hit the road again.

As the sun began to set, casting long shadows across the desert, I could feel the fatigue setting in. I made another stop, this time at a larger station with a small diner attached. The waitress, a middle-aged woman with a no-nonsense demeanor, served me a sandwich and coffee.

"Long trip?" she asked, her eyes curious but kind.

"Yeah," I said, taking a bite of the sandwich. "Just passing through."

"Well, take care out there," she replied, refilling my coffee cup. "The desert can be a dull yet dangerous place alone at night."

I nodded, grateful for her concern. After finishing my meal, I got back on the road, the Packard's headlights cutting through the encroaching darkness. The miles rolled by, the desert landscape bathed in the pale light of the rising moon, cacti glittering.

As I neared Las Vegas, the air grew cooler, the desert's heat giving way to a chill that crept in with the night. The city emerged like a mirage, a cluster of lights in the middle of the vast, empty expanse. In 1939, Las Vegas was far from the neon-lit spectacle it would become, but it had a unique charm all its own.

I found a modest motel on the outskirts of town and checked in. The clerk, a young man with a bored expression, handed me a key without much interest. The room was small and simple, a bed and a dresser with a mirror. I took a quick shower, washing away the dust and grime of the road, then ventured out into the city.

Las Vegas had a raw, untamed feel to it. The streets were alive with activity, people moving to and fro with an energy that was almost palpable. I found a small café and ordered a meal, enjoying the simple pleasure of hot food and fresh coffee. The waiter, a friendly man in his thirties, recommended a visit to the Hoover Dam.

"It's quite a sight," he said, placing my plate in front of me. "Worth the trip if you've got the time."

I nodded, deciding to take his advice. After finishing my meal, I returned to the motel and fell into a deep sleep, the day's journey catching up with me.

The next morning, I woke early, eager to explore before continuing my journey. The drive to the Hoover Dam was short, the road winding through the rugged terrain. As I approached, the dam rose up before me, an impressive feat of engineering carved out of the rock. I parked the Packard and walked to the viewing area, the massive structure looming over the Colorado River below.

The sight was breathtaking, a testament to human ingenuity and determination. I stood there for a long time, taking in the sheer scale of the dam, the way it held back the river's power. These were sights I would never see again, moments of awe and wonder that punctuated the relentless march of my journey.

As I wandered around the site, I couldn't help but think of the people who had built it, the thousands of workers who had toiled under the harsh sun to create something enduring. Their legacy stood before me, a symbol of perseverance and resilience.

After spending a few hours at the dam, I returned to Las Vegas and found a small diner for a quick lunch. The waitress, a young woman with a bright smile, served me a sandwich and a fresh cup of coffee.

"Passing through?" She asked, making small talk.

"Sure am, heading west," I replied, my standard answer.

"Well, enjoy your stay," she said cheerfully. I thanked her and finished my meal, then headed back to the Packard.

I grew more excited when I got back on the road from Las Vegas. It may have been more desert, was long and desolate, but that did nothing to dampen my spirits.

A few hours later was yet another stop for fuel . This time, it was a lonely station run by an older man with a friendly demeanor.

"Which way you headed?" He asked, pumping gas into the tank.

"California," I said, handing over the cash.

"Ah, not so far from here," he remarked, handing me my change. I nodded, grabbing a coffee from the station's small counter. It was strong and bitter, but it would keep me awake.

As I drove, the landscape began to change again. The desert gave way to rolling hills and then to the rugged mountains of the Sierra Nevada. The miles passed slowly, each one a reminder of how far I'd come and how far I still had to go.

As the sun dipped below the horizon, casting elongated shadows over the landscape, I approached the outskirts of another small town. I found a modest motel and checked in, the clerk giving me a curious look but saying nothing. The room was basic but comfortable, a haven for the night. I took a quick shower and collapsed onto the bed, exhaustion finally catching up with me.

I woke with the first rays of light that streamed through the curtains.

I packed my things and hit the road again. The Packard roared to life, eager to continue the journey.

Back on the open road, my thoughts drifted to the days when flying was my passion, my escape. Each stop was a bittersweet reminder of how far I'd traveled, both in miles and in life. I kept a mental map of every town, every gas station, each one a small marker of progress in this arduous journey. Glendale awaited, and with it, the final chapter of my plan.

The highway stretched out ahead, an endless ribbon of asphalt. The Packard devoured the miles, each one a small victory against the vast expanse of the American landscape. Small towns flashed by, their names quickly forgotten, each with its own story and charm. But I wasn't here to admire them; I had a mission, and that mission drove me forward relentlessly.

Driving through Las Vegas had been a stark reminder of my purpose. The brief respite to see the Hoover Dam was a moment of clarity, a chance to remember what I was truly fighting for. Now, it was just me and the road. The mission was my only companion, my singular focus. I was Amelia Earhart, and nothing could stand in my way.

The Packard's engine roared as the miles rolled under its wheels. I navigated through landscapes that varied from barren deserts to lush hills. Each town I passed through was a dot on my mental map, a testament to the distance I had covered. The journey was grueling, but every drop of gasoline and every cup of coffee propelled me closer to Glendale.

This journey had taken me from the serene plains of Toledo to the bustling streets of Des Moines, and through the towering mountains of Denver. Each place had offered a brief respite, a moment of normalcy in a world that felt increasingly distant. Now, Las Vegas had given me another brief interlude, a snapshot of a city on the verge of transformation.

As I approached my final destination, the road seemed to stretch on indefinitely, an endless ribbon of possibilities and memories. Each fuel stop was a checkpoint, each cup of coffee a lifeline. The Packard continued to eat up the miles, but now each one felt more significant, more meaningful. The end was in sight, and with it, the culmination of everything I had fought for.

Glendale was waiting, and with it, the resolution to a journey that had taken me across the heartland of America. The road had been long and challenging, but every mile had brought me closer to my goal. The Packard roared on, and I knew that nothing could stop me now. I was Amelia Earhart, and I was unstoppable.

Thirty-One

Leaving Las Vegas behind, I felt a renewed sense of purpose. The neon lights faded in my rearview mirror as the Packard 120 ate up the miles. Glendale was calling, and I was answering.

The desert stretched out before me, a vast expanse of sand and scrub under the relentless sun. My hands gripped the steering wheel, knuckles white with determination. This was the final leg of my journey, and nothing would stop me now.

I'd been running for so long, it felt strange to be heading toward something instead of away. But Glendale held answers, and I needed them desperately.

The road shimmered in the heat, a mirage of water always just out of reach. It reminded me of my days in the air, when the horizon seemed to stretch on forever. Now, my world had shrunk to the size of this car, this ribbon of asphalt cutting through the desert.

Hours passed in a blur of cacti and tumbleweeds. The sun arced across the sky, casting long shadows as afternoon turned to evening. I stopped only when necessary, for fuel and coffee strong enough to strip paint.

At one such stop, a wizened old man with skin like leather eyed me curiously. "You're a long way from home, miss," he said, his voice as dry as the surrounding landscape.

I nodded, not bothering to correct him. Home was a concept I'd left behind long ago. "Just passing through," I replied, my standard response.

He grunted, handing me my change. "Well, watch yourself out there. Desert's no place for a lady alone."

I bit back a sharp retort. If only he knew who I really was, what I'd been through. Instead, I simply smiled tightly and got back on the road.

As night fell, the temperature dropped rapidly. The desert's heat gave way to a bone-deep chill that crept in through the Packard's windows. I pulled over briefly to grab a jacket from my bag, shrugging it on without taking my eyes off the road.

The stars came out, a dazzling array that took my breath away. Out here, away from the city lights, the Milky Way stretched across the sky like a river of diamonds. It made me ache for my flying days, when I'd felt closer to those stars than to the earth below.

But those days were gone, replaced by this new reality of endless roads and fleeting identities. I was Amelia Earhart, yes, but I was also a ghost, a woman who should be dead. The irony wasn't lost on me.

As midnight approached, fatigue began to set in. My eyes felt gritty, and the white lines on the road started to blur. I knew I needed to stop, but the thought of delaying my arrival in Glendale even by a few hours was unbearable.

I pushed on, fueled by determination and the dregs of my last cup of coffee. The Packard's headlights cut through the darkness, illuminating a world that seemed to consist solely of cacti and rocks.

Just when I thought I couldn't go any further, I saw lights on the horizon. A small town materialized out of the darkness, a welcome oasis in the desert night.

I pulled into the first motel I saw, a run-down place with a flickering neon sign. The night clerk barely looked up from his magazine as he handed me a key. The room was basic but clean, and at that moment, it looked like the Ritz.

I collapsed onto the bed, not bothering to undress. Sleep claimed me almost instantly, dreamless and deep.

Morning came too soon, sunlight streaming through the thin curtains. I groaned, every muscle protesting as I forced myself to sit up. A quick glance at my watch told me I'd slept for barely four hours.

It would have to do. Glendale was waiting.

I splashed some water on my face, ran a comb through my hair, and checked out. The same clerk was still there, looking as though he hadn't moved all night. He grunted a goodbye as I left.

Back on the road, the desert looked different in the early morning light. The rising sun painted the landscape in shades of gold and pink, softening the harsh edges of the previous day.

I drove with renewed energy, knowing that each mile brought me closer to my goal. The Packard responded eagerly, as if it too sensed the importance of our destination.

As the morning wore on, the terrain began to change. The flat desert gave way to rolling hills, and in the distance, I could see the faint outline of mountains. California was getting closer.

I stopped for gas at a small station just across the state line. The attendant, a young man with a friendly smile, chatted as he filled the tank.

"Where you headed?" He asked.

"Glendale," I replied, surprising myself with my honesty.

He whistled. "That's quite a drive. You must be eager to get there."

I nodded, not trusting myself to speak. Eager didn't begin to cover it. I was drawn to Glendale like a moth to a flame, knowing it could be my salvation or my destruction.

Back on the road, I let my mind wander to what awaited me in Glendale. Would anyone recognize me? If they did, how would, or should, I react? Tell them I heard that I looked like Amelia all the time? The uncertainty gnawed at me, but there was no turning back now.

The mountains loomed larger as I approached, their snow-capped peaks a stark contrast to the desert I'd left behind. The air grew cooler, and I rolled down the windows to let in the fresh mountain breeze.

As I wound my way through the mountain passes, I couldn't help but think of my flying days. The thrill of navigating through cloud-shrouded peaks, the exhilaration of emerging into clear skies. Now, earthbound, I felt a pang of loss for that freedom.

But I pushed those thoughts aside. This journey wasn't about reliving past glories. It was about securing a future, about finally putting to rest the ghosts that had been chasing me for so long.

The descent into the Los Angeles basin was like entering another world. The landscape changed dramatically, lush greenery replacing the arid desert. And then, suddenly, there were buildings everywhere, roads crisscrossing in a dizzying network.

My heart raced as I saw the sign: "Glendale 20 miles." I was so close now, I could almost taste it.

The traffic grew heavier as I approached the city. It was a shock after the empty desert roads, and I had to focus intently to navigate the unfamiliar streets. The Packard, so steady on the open road, felt unwieldy in this urban maze.

Finally, I saw it: "Welcome to Glendale." I'd made it.

But now that I was here, uncertainty gripped me. I knew where I was going and who I was going to see. I even knew what I would be doing once I got there. Yet I was still uncertain.

About what? You know exactly what to do.

I pulled over to the side of the road, ignoring the annoyed honks of passing cars.

"Do I? I don't know what I'll use to do it..."

And the tire iron in the trunk simply won't do. Hmm...

I parked the Packard and got out, stretching my cramped muscles. The sound of a plane taking off in the distance made me look up instinctively, shading my eyes against the sun.

We stayed on the side of the road for a while, watching the planes take off from the airfield nearby.

Then it hit me.

Thirty-Two

I JUMPED BACK INTO the Packard, excited for what was next.

Amelia, would you mind sharing what the fuss is all about?

"As soon as I get back out into traffic," I replied.

A few minutes later, I was cruising along, headed to the closest airplane hangar and shop I knew of.

We're headed to a hangar, I see. But what's there?

"All pilots carry survival knives."

Okay. And?

"And they keep them sharpened, just in case."

I dodged in and out of cars who were driving along lazily. I had things to do and people to...talk to.

Ah. Now I get it.

"Glad you're back with me," I replied with a smirk.

Parking in the lot of the hangar, I watched for the one man inside to leave. As soon as he was gone, I jumped out of the driver's seat and jogged into the shop.

I got lucky and didn't even have to dig around for the survival knife, which was a big no-no in the industry. We usually kept them on our persons. This guy must have felt comfortable enough to just leave it sitting on the workbench. I pocketed it and took off back to my waiting sedan. That was the last rush I'd get.

The traffic on the way to Forest Lawn was mostly light. There were some spots that had backed up frequently when I was alive, and they still did now, but with more cars. Not that I expected two years to make as much of a difference as it had.

I drove through the gates of Forest Lawn about an hour after stealing the survival knife. I was finally able to breathe again, as though I'd been holding it since I left Las Vegas.

There were many hills in this cemetery, and I needed to go over three of them to get to my end point. When I did, I shut the car off and exited, leaving the keys in the ignition before grabbing my journal and closing the door.

I walked slowly, journal held in front of me in both hands. I slowed to a crawl as I got closer to the marker. When I reached it, I dropped to my knees.

"Father..."

I broke into tears. I was neither sad nor remorseful. I was simply releasing the weight of who I'd been and who I was now.

"Father," I started again, "I'm here. I apologize for Amy and Muriel's horrible behavior toward you. You were the only one who didn't try to change me. For that I am grateful."

I placed the journal on top of the marker.

"There are many letters to you inside."

Then I picked up the survival knife, admiring the sharpness of it, and smiled.

"Edwin, today I join you. There is no point to my survival anymore. If I stayed, I'd surely go to jail for the things I've done."

I poked at my jugular with the knife tip, drawing blood from the flesh wound.

"Goodbye, father. Or is it hello?"

At that, I stabbed clear through my jugular, spouting blood onto the journal and all over my clothes. I slumped further down, and finally lay on the grass, gurgling. I was finally at peace with myself and my decisions. At peace with my life.

I am Amelia Earhart and I am a serial killer.

The world went black.

Also by Amanda Byrd

13 Reasons for Murder:

Politeness Kills (#1)

Meathead (#2)

Philistines (#3)

Hungry (#4)

Bad Blood (#5)

Betrayal (#6)

Disillusioned (#7)

Harlot (#8)

The Morgan Davis Serials

The Girl at the Bottom of the Ocean (#1)

Before You Die (#2)

Serial Women of History
Amelia Earhart, Serial Killer

www.ingramcontent.com/pod-product-compliance
Lightning Source LLC
Chambersburg PA
CBHW061809190726

48289CB00007B/2136